The
Trove

Tobias S. Buckell

DEDICATION

The Trove was created via the generous backing of readers who joined together on Kickstarter to make this book a reality. Some went above and beyond the call of duty. This book is dedicated to the enthusiasm and support of:

Chris McLaren
Garth Nix
AMD 'Doc' Hamm
and Clare Bohn

Chapter One

With a gust of cold air, the doors to the inn my two mothers and I lived in slid open, and the rigger stepped inside.

I knew he was a rigger because he had those eye implants that only riggers wore. Infinite-black goggles that had been welded to the outer flesh of his eye sockets, the surfaces pitted dull from radiation and micro-abrasions.

He was a thin, skeletal thing with surgical scarring up and down his face. Underneath his transparent, paper-like skin you could see embedded machines and odd shaped chunks of metal. Patterns that hinted at things inside him that could control the complex, rapid machinery of sparships a mile long, ghosting through the cold depths of space.

I smiled when I saw him because the men who plied the inky depths of the space between suns were mysterious, and maybe a little dangerous when you saw them in person. It was a combination that promised to bring some excitement into my boring routine.

I welcomed it. I was normally supposed to call Sadayya down to the fake marble countertop of the inn's reception desk when a guest arrived, so she could handle everything while I watched and learned. But I knew how to check in a guest myself. I quickly decided I'd 'forget' to call her.

This rigger's bald skull gleamed in the streetlamp light. In the cool air that wafted inside with him, I could see ripples of heat rising from his scalp. The circuits and machines that supercharged his very brain created too much waste heat.

A rigger with more money than this man would have afforded better implants that didn't look so mechanical. He would have artificial eyes that looked real. Before me was a cobbled together patchwork of machine and man, and a well-weathered one at that.

5

"There we are," he said in a voice that sounded like rocks run across a grater, looking around the common room of the Inn. He waved a hand, and a series of dilapidated spider-like robots with oddly jointed arms staggered out from behind him carrying a giant trunk. The onyx-black sheen of the trunk's exterior soaked up any light that touched it, it was like a square black hole. "You have rooms large enough to store my trunk, yes?"

The trunk, which was maybe ten feet long, hissed some kind of cold, superconductive fog out of broken vents. It was old and beaten up, scarred in some places. And whatever it was, with cooling fog like that, it probably contained enough computing power to run a small city. It certainly had more refrigeration capability than the deep freeze in our kitchen.

I was insanely curious about it.

"Welcome to the Nelson Inn," I said, greeting the rigger.

This was the personal touch, as Sadayya liked to say when she taught me how to check our guests in. Something few people got to experience anymore when houses that could speak and think usually handled such mundane things.

Sadayya usually left the desk and touched a customer's arm as she spoke. But I was a bit intimidated by the large rigger and stayed behind the desk. Besides, I needed to use the manual screen behind the desk to check him in.

It didn't really matter where Sadayya would have stood, though, as she could book their room anywhere with a few taps in the air, or even by talking to the Inn. The Inn's various computers and circuits combined to the point it was almost intelligent, able to understand basic phrases, as well as run the Inn's internal infrastructure. As a child it had even read stories to me, in order to increase my verbal intelligence. Old, copyright-free tales about princesses and ponies and crap like that, which it thought I would enjoy.

In a word, boring stuff.

To be fair to the Inn it had quickly consulted with an educational specialist, and after some interviews with me about my preferences, served me up with tall tales of adventurers and

The Trove

history. Blood and guts and swashbuckling. Tales about fights between riggers and aliens. Or even the showdown with the menace of the *Sparkflint*, when all of Earth was threatened by a vast sparship the size of a small world and its insanely murderous crew. I would listen any day to the legend that the *Sparkflint* itself was inhabited by an experimental artificial mind gone insane.

Anything but stories about people stuck in castles.

Boring.

I lived on a medium-sized floating city, in an Inn perched near a small space launch facility. In other words, I lived in a complete and utter dead end where almost nothing ever happened. It was much more exciting to read about people who roved other worlds, and escaped their humble surroundings.

"Jane Hawkins!" Sadayya appeared at the bottom of the stairs and hissed at me. Like any other mother, the use of my full name meant she was more than a little angry at me. "You're supposed to let me know when a guest comes in. The Inn had to tell me!"

Her lips were tight with annoyance, and I didn't try to come up with anything other than a half shrug. "You were upstairs," I said. "You shouldn't be bothered when you're upstairs. I can help out more. I help out enough as it is…"

It was a statement just true enough that her anger deflated. And there was, after all, a guest standing right there.

She pivoted to give him her attention.

"I'm Sadayya Hawkins," my mother introduced herself. She tried to shake the man's hand now that she stood in front of him, but that was a planet-side habit. Men like this rigger lived their lives in carefully scrubbed air and compartments, and they did not like germs.

Least of all, germy hands.

My mother's attempt to shake his hand was ignored, so she pretended as if nothing had happened and continued. "And your name is?" she asked.

"I need power. And I need a large room," was all the

7

mysterious new guest said, gruffly.

He stalked through our small lobby and looked out
through the panorama windows at the nearby space port. The
Nelson Inn perched on an artificial metal cliff of apartments, a
warren of humanity that was too poor to live on the surface of
the city, or who could afford the stunning vistas that came if
you lived on the very edge of the floating city. Many of us
huddled near the pit-like spaceport in the north corner, where it
was cheap due to the noise, or lived in the underground
apartments.

My mothers said that if we were so close to the space
port, then we might as well make our worst feature the best:
from the Inn you could look out on the spires and terminals of
the port. You could see the occasional mile-long ship fold their
spars down against their hulls and ease into their berths.

Most people hated living near the rumble and groan of
that traffic. Even if the Sargasso port was a lesser visited port.
Fewer people still wanted to stay in an Inn near all that. Mostly
our guests were down on their luck, or moving through.
Waiting for a launch the next morning.

"I want a room facing the port," the rigger demanded.
Which was unusual, because men like him rarely wanted to see
anything but ships and ports.

Giving him a room facing the port would be easy. Almost
all our rooms were empty. Business was slow.

My mother stood there, waiting. The rigger smiled slowly
and snapped his fingers at her. It must have triggered a
payment as my mother looked at the empty space in the air
where he had snapped, tapped the air, and nodded.

If Sadayya had let me get chipped, I would have been able
to see icons hanging in the air as the rigger paid for his room
and board. I could have seen the receipt Sadayya gave him, or
even Sadayya's own customer profile information.

I would have been able to see information the Inn
projected to all of our grownup guests and much more,
particularly when outside. The world was riddled with layers of
information that enhanced eyes and enhanced brains could see.

Augmented realities, created by all sorts of computers and wireless networks talking to each other and meshing people in. But I was too young. Sadayya only let me see some of it with a clunky pair of glasses that I could put on. But interacting with everything required talking to the dumb glasses, which weren't even as smart as the somewhat helpful, but often moronic, Inn.

Once, when my mothers were young, they said intelligent computers would help us do everything. But ever since the AI that ran the sparship *Sparkflint* turned on Earth itself, strong artificial intelligences had become highly regulated. Or outright banned.

"That'll pay for the night, and then some," the mysterious rigger said as he absently waved at a spider near his feet. It scuttled back away from him.

"I'm telling the Inn to recognize you as a guest and have assigned you to a room. It will guide you to it."

The man nodded, and he must now be seeing the Inn's map to his room, because he waved the spiders on. In addition to carrying the black slab of his trunk, they had bags with fist sized camera lenses and communications equipment.

All of this the mechanical spiders struggled to carry up the steep stairs past me. And with the air of a general ordering his troops forward, the rigger walked behind them, urging the mindless metal contraptions on.

"Who are you?" I asked as he passed me by, giving me a whiff of burnt live wires and plastic. I tried to learn the guest's names and, when I could, their stories. I loved to listen to riggers talk about the ships they worked on. Vehicles that blasted away from this world, from this backwater city, at speeds so fast light drooped around them. There were whole worlds outside the Inn. I collected them, like a bird bringing shiny things back to its nest. "I'm Jane. Jane Hawkins."

"Call me Captain," he murmured as he brushed past.

And then, with much chattering and rattling, the entire army finished storming the stairs. At the top, the rigger 'Captain' turned and glanced back down, as if he were worried that he was being followed.

"What did his background check show?" I asked Sadayya casually. And then, in a lecturing tone, "You know we're required to check all our guests. And this one won't even tell me his name. Did he tell *you* his name?"

Sadayya was always telling me I needed to learn the legal aspects of being an Innkeeper, as one day I would fully run it. If you didn't ping someone's profile, then you didn't know if they were safe guests, with clean backgrounds and recommendations from other Innkeepers.

"He prefers an anonymous profile, but it is a good one with a unique key. The Inn is still hunting. He hasn't spent much time on Earth. It will take time for the accounts to synchronize his off-Earth profiles." Sadayya shrugged. "He paid in full and the money is in our account, that is all that matters right now. We need it. He might look strange, Jane, but remember, riggers have to modify their bodies to live in space and work on their ships. It doesn't mean that there is anything wrong with them. I doubt we'll find out anything negative about his profile. Riggers just like their privacy."

"Sure they do," I said.

But I remembered the expression on the man's face as he glanced back down the stairs. It was the same look a fox would throw over their shoulder, making sure they'd left the hounds on the other side of the river.

Well, if foxes hadn't gone extinct, I thought.

Chapter Two

I watched the 'Captain' stride out of the Inn. I'd just finished my chores when I saw him pound down the stairs. I grabbed my special scarf, wrapped the ratty, yellow and black fabric around my neck, and followed him out onto the street. The fake brick and plastic facades of neon-lit storefronts choked the alleys behind the Inn, and it took a second for my eyes to adjust as I looked around.

After his dramatic entrance, our new guest had mostly kept to himself for the next day or two. Much to my disappointment.

Now he was on the move. Following him would be a nice break from the Inn.

A bitter wind cut at my neck as I shadowed the rigger. Our floating city, Sargasso, made a regular circuit over the Atlantic Ocean and we were in the polar route of the yearly trip. The city had just ambled on past Greenland. Ice crystalized and drooped from the retro-decorative streetlights I slipped around.

I hated that. Most floating cities migrated south for the winters. Our city owners, however, liked the change in seasons, and so the rest of us got dragged through the icy cold.

The rigger, not used to the idea of unregulated weather, purchased a large, heated overcoat from a nearby outerwear store to keep warm for what became a long walk around the snow-dappled streets of Sargasso.

We slid from the packed retail clusters near the Inn, down into the underground. No sky overhead, just the metallic underbelly of the city's basement. Fluorescent light glared, and people packed the corridors that ran under the streets.

I followed him deeper into the city's center, into the shades, where the lights flickered out and people stopped nodding at each other.

I realized that the rigger was looking to score in order to slow himself down. Those chips in his brain that dumped heat into the air over his head kept his mind sped up so that he could handle helping fly a sparship. Because of that amped nervous system, riggers were always jittery. They moved around like giant hummingbirds.

But they craved slowing down into the normal world with the rest of us. Most of them didn't have the expensive hardware that could downclock their minds safely, so they dangerously slowed themselves in other ways.

This usually involved a cocktail of various drugs. Downers, all of them. Many of them prescribed by shady pharmacies deep in Sargasso. The drugs would drag a rigger all the way down, until they were relaxed, calm, and well out of it. Sometimes near the spaceports I found them lying in chairs and drooling: happy to be near-stupid.

I was disappointed that this man was like so many of the others who came through our Inn.

When we returned to the Inn, he paused and glanced at the handful of other guests in the lobby. I slipped in after him, right before the doors closed. Again, I saw that nervous look on his face that I'd seen when he was at the top of the stairs.

"Jane Hawkins," he said, without turning back to look at me. "How long have you been following me?"

I froze. *Damn.* I'd been caught.

He still had his back to me. "You see everything that goes on here, don't you? Got your eye on the whole place, know the nooks and crannies of that street outside, do ya?"

"I see things," I said, nervous. "Are you going to tell my mothers?"

"No. In fact, I want you to do me a favor," he said in his gravelly voice. He turned around now, his black, machine eyes looking at me. "See them?"

He pointed outside at a crew of young riggers with purple and gray heat-dissipating metal mohawks glinting in the neon light. They walked up the street on their way to a nearby club, laughing and shoving each other.

"You ever see three riggers moving together, like they're one, you send me a message," he hissed. And strangely, he seemed more nervous than I was. "You *warn* me."

"What's it worth to you?" I asked promptly, even though the black eyepatches made me shiver.

He laughed at my audacity.

"I'll give you anonymous credit chips. Use them anywhere, for anything." He scratched his cheek. "I'm sure that's something your parents wouldn't be handing you, yeah?"

I held out a hand. He snorted, dug around in the pockets of a utility vest, and pulled out a shiny black chit. I reached for it, but he pulled his hand away so fast it blurred.

He leaned in close enough that I could smell his chemical sweat.

"You watch out for the three of them that walk like they're one person, *then* you'll get paid."

I swallowed, a little bit terrified, but a little bit insulted. "I spend all that time watching and nothing happens, then you don't pay me? Why would I be stupid enough to do that?"

The rigger tried to stare me down. To intimidate me. So I gave the black, eye-patched stare a blast of a defiantly raised eyebrow. He relented with a skeevy smile that grew out of his scowl. "Here's half," he growled. And then, with sudden curiosity. "What's your trick?"

"My trick?" I palmed the chit and thought about where I was going to have to hide it so that Sadayya never found it.

"I didn't see you outside. Didn't notice you until the door didn't close right away. How did you do it?"

A triumphant flush swirled through me. "I'm invisible," I told him playfully.

"How?"

I was in the mood to show off. I rewrapped the yellow and black scarf around my neck and traced the controls woven into its edges.

"There's a program embedded in the scarf. If your eyes are chipped, or your brain, I can use that against you. The scarf spoofs what people see, makes me look like I'm part of whatever's around. It doesn't work with everyone, children see me, of course. Or ,I could see me," I said a little bitterly. "But a rigger like you... it works well enough. The trick is to stay absolutely still to remain out of sight. Just one tiny muscle movement, and the processors can't keep up with the illusion, and it'll break apart."

For a moment he looked fascinated. "You can remain that still?"

"I practice. The Inn reads me Zen meditation guides. The scarf was broken when I found it for sale, and I spent months getting it fixed to work again. My mother, Tia, helped."

And that was all I would say, because I didn't like talking about Tia to strangers. The wave of sadness that came with that suddenly made the little adventure I'd undertaken spoil.

"Don't do it around me ever again," the rigger said, suddenly calm, but his voice forceful. He was angry. "You watch out for the three, then you'll get the rest of your pay."

He stomped up the stairs and shut himself into his room.

Three riggers that walked as one. I wasn't even sure what that meant. It was probably just the side effect of some brain-damaged paranoia of his. These were men who saw things almost unimaginable to those of us who lived on Earth. And they were human, but so changed, so modified, that they were almost unhuman. Or maybe inhuman.

They moved wrong, looked wrong, and yet they were men.

Men who saw and did things I could only dream of.

And that had to affect you. Along with all those tiny chips, and computers that added to their brain functions.

I thought about that later while watching him at the tiny lobby bar with three other riggers who'd come in for a single night at the Inn. They all ordered drinks from the robotic mixer. They were all doped up on downers so hard they moved slowly and deliberately, as if the air in the Inn had turned to honey.

One of the riggers told a loud story about pulling in a ship's spars, battening in to skim the rim of a black hole itself.

And another jumped in to talk about a fight between ships that were light years apart.

The 'Captain' smiled knowingly to himself.

As if those things were nothing compared to the things he had seen.

***

Three days later I found our new guest collapsed on the lobby floor, unable to move, his eyeless face turned to the ceiling as his hands twitched. Drool spilled out of the corner of his mouth and dribbled on the floor, and his nose bled down his ashy lips.

He'd overdosed on downers.

I screamed for the Inn to call a mobile medic, sure that he was dying right there on the high-traffic carpet.

The emergency medical drone that arrived looked like a mechanical wasp the size of my forearm. It flew right through our doors and perched on the guest's chest. The stinger, a multi-barreled set of syringes and scalpels, hesitated as the insect eyes of the drone scanned the still form with a beam of blue light.

But the rigger raised a hand and knocked the drone away. It flew up into the air and hung still.

"No permission," the guest mumbled. "Leave me alone."

"You have refused treatment," the drone said tonelessly to the guest. "Your bill for the call and the scan will arrive shortly."

By the time Sadayya came down the stairs, the rigger was stumbling up them, repeating himself. "Leave me alone." He shoved past her and hid in his room.

I looked at Sadayya, who blinked and rubbed her eyes. They were puffy, with black marks underneath. She hadn't been sleeping well. Not for months.

She didn't even ask what had happened, she just turned around and went back up to Tia's room with her shoulders slumped.

***

The rigger started off with transdermal patches to slow down. He would slap one against the side of his neck with a deep sigh. But by the end of the week he returned from his long, cold walks with small blue tubes of compressed drugs. He'd hold one injector against the forearm or neck and trigger it to shoot a dose of zen-like calm directly into his bloodstream.

I'd seen enough riggers around to know they took to the blue stuff like a kid to candy.

Some of the locals who visited our bar, who normally huddled away in the dark of the honeycomb warrens under the buildings and streets, tried to pry more and more interesting stories out of him for fun. If the rigger was mellowed out enough he'd talk loudly about rogue mind-viruses that took you over to use as spare computing units. Or about the Kai Hanimar, and the way they'd flayed any riggers they found in their trading triangles and broadcast the videos of the horrible deed to any human who came near Kai Hanimar trade routes.

But more often he was too naturally keyed up from his rigger implants to keep his thoughts straight. He was just as likely to start shouting at us in half-completed bursts of profanity rather than complete a story.

I started tiptoeing around him. And locals stopped coming to the bar.

He made people nervous. Some because they didn't want to think about the wars and riggers. Others because they were sure he would turn violent.

Sadayya initiated eviction procedures, but the rigger had a legal artificial mind working on his behalf. The case got tied up in municipal court.

We became resigned to our now unwanted guest.

***

Dr. Armstrong came to check on Tia that weekend.

Afterwards, he came down to the lobby with Sadayya. They both looked grim, and somewhat exhausted.

Dr. Armstrong had known my mothers for a long time. Tia told me once that the Armstrong had stayed in the Inn when he first came to Sargasso. That was before he had his license, and before he'd inherited a lot of money that allowed him to take classes and invest in medical neural upgrades and training.

Back then he'd lived like us: close to the airport and just above the city's underground warrens.

Now he sat at a table and showed Sadayya the treatments and options for Tia. I knew to leave them alone when it was like this. And I knew what the whispers and worried faces meant. It was that hint of the thunderstorm on the horizon.

But as they murmured to each other, the rigger wandered into the lobby while mumbling, shouting, and waving at the air, deep into some hallucination or flashback.

Dr. Armstrong paused and then stood up. I knew the doctor had implants to help him use instruments, but I wondered if they let him move as quickly as I'd seen the rigger move.

"You're overdoing it," Dr. Armstrong said firmly. "And you're bothering us."

The doctor got a sideways glance, though it was always hard to tell with those black, featureless ovoids welded over the rigger's eyes. "I'm none of your business," the rigger said.

"You know you'll kill yourself, trying to hold yourself down like that. You'll break. That when it comes time to try and get past the addiction, you'll be useless."

"You don't know what it's like to live a million miles a second, little man," was the gravelly reply. "While juggling the infinite variables required to make the right choices to keep a ship on the line and moving between the stars. You have *no idea*. I could strike you down before you even could comprehend what was happening. You understand *that*? I'm that quick."

"Strike *me* down? I'm a standing member of the city's

council! I can have Sargasso Security down here within the minute," Dr. Armstrong snapped. "You threaten me again, or anyone else here, and you *will* find yourself banned from these streets. Hell, I'll personally help throw you over the side of the city if you keep bothering people in this Inn. Do you understand?"

For a long moment they faced each other, staring each other down, and then the rigger started scratching at his cheek and mumbling to himself again.

The peace held as he retreated to his room and left us alone, and for a while things got a little better.

But not for long.

Chapter Three

The city of Sargasso moved further north into the Arctic, bringing an even more bitter chill and too much snow to the streets. The ice dripped from the skyscrapers of the central district, and the jet-stream reached down out of the upper atmosphere to rip down through our steel canyoned streets.

I was at the desk when the rigger clumped down the stairs, pulling on his thermal overcoat closely around him.

"You can't go out," I said.

"Why?" he growled, walking for the doors.

"Snow." I pointed at one of the automated snow trucks outside, headed towards the edge of the city to dump ice over the side. "Too much ice and snow across the city. There are instabilities in the city's balance. Municipal services sent out a travel ban."

For the next day we'd be stuck inside, edgy and festering in each other's company.

The rigger snorted and walked out into the cold. He disappeared into a flurry of snow kicked up by the edge of an automated plow.

"Was that the rigger?" Sadayya asked from up the stairs. "Did you tell him there's a travel ban?"

I sighed. "Yes, of course I did." It wasn't like I'd opened the door and shoved him out against his will.

"You should come upstairs. Leave the desk. No one's coming in today. The Inn can take care of it."

I didn't want to go upstairs, and that made me feel like a horrible person. I didn't talk about it, either. I certainly tried not to think about it. In a way, working at the Inn helped. Because it was easier to keep what was happening separate. I kept what was happening upstairs in the private section of our Inn cordoned off in another portion of my mind.

The rot had been eating away at Tia for a long time now. An advanced degenerative neural disease that Dr. Armstrong couldn't do anything for. But the end crept close to us now. She had been spending more and more of her time inside the medical capsule upstairs that monitored and attempted to stabilize her condition, hardly able to get out and move.

I could stand over the glass and put my hand to it. That's as much contact with her as I'd had for months, now.

It wasn't good enough. It wasn't fair.

At least down here, I could *do* something.

"I have to clean up after breakfast," I shouted back up to her.

There was a pause. Then Sadayya said, "Clean. Then come upstairs."

I waited until I heard the door shut, then walked out to the bar and eating area. The bright lighting seemed out of place when the cold gloom outside was trying to reach into the lobby and squeeze everything inside into a sort of dreary gray.

One of the rigger's spiders sat in an alcove. A telephoto camera lens had been strapped onto its carapace, and it sat at the window, spying at the space port.

Creepy.

I was almost done cleaning the small breakfast buffet when the doors to the Inn opened with a blast of shivery air. I turned away from dishes of date-filled pastries, fresh fruit, and flat bread. I expected to see our rigger, but it wasn't him.

The stranger's left arm was a tangled mess of flesh and robotics carefully wrapped in a plastic guard. Her face was stretched taught, with four, perfect black cuts above each cheek almost near the sides of her silvered eyes.

Another rigger.

Apparently they all felt city rules didn't apply to them.

She sat near the buffet. She didn't order a room, or ask for food. She just sat there silently, her metallic eyes tracking every move I made as I cleaned up.

I finally had enough of this, and wrung my cleaning rag out. I turned and walked over to her table. "How can I help you?" I asked, each word of mine as crisp and cold as the frosted air she'd dragged in.

She sort of leered at me, the silver eyes darting around the room. "Hello young lady. I'm looking for a good friend. Villem. I was supposed to meet him here, but…" she laughed in an odd manner. Almost as if saying the words 'hahaha' instead of actually chuckling them.

"Our guests' privacy is important to the Nelson Inn." I said as I crossed my arms and looked down my nose at her. "I can take a message for a guest if you leave one. *If* they're even here."

The woman said 'hahaha' again, and raised her plastic-encased arm. "Villem might be calling himself by another name, yes? He's a tricky one. But he'll be hitting the downers, because Villem's sped up. Sped up hard. So… see anyone leaving little blue tubes around? Maybe someone with dark oversocket implants? Then you know him, yeah?"

"I couldn't say," I lied. "But if there is such a man, what would you like me to tell him?"

The woman's face twisted with anger, and she grabbed one of my elbows with her half mechanical arm so hard it hurt. She pulled me closer with a rough yank. She pointed with her other hand over at the viewing windows where the spidery robot with the camera sat. "I see one of Villem's crappy, half worn-out drones right in the open there, girl. Now where the hell is he?"

"He's not here right now," I said, not seeing the point in covering for the guest rigger anymore. "Now please let go of me."

"I have a daughter, too," she said, ignoring me. "So I don't want to hurt you. I will let go of you. But you will stay in this room and remain quiet. Try to call for help, try to do anything, and there *will* be trouble for you."

I sprang up when she let go of my elbow, and so did she. She pulled out a wicked long gun with clamps where a grip usually was. And when she let it go it slithered onto her hand and fastened itself into place like a stick insect wrapping its legs around a branch.

She patted me on my shoulder. "I like your hair," she muttered. "And you are well tanned, you spend a lot of time in the sun. Or maybe you're like that naturally. Hard to tell. But those locks must have taken a long time to grow... you don't see dreadlocks much in space, you know, they float around too much when you're in zero gravity. On a ship with Villem, yeah, you wouldn't dare let your hair go long. No, Villem wasn't the type. All discipline and order on his ship. Always made me shave *my* hair. Always the captain. Did he tell you he was a captain?"

I said nothing.

The rigger paid no attention to my silence, though. "It'll be good to surprise Villem, good to see him," she continued on, as if trying to talk herself into believing it.

As we waited she kept trying to act as if she was making a friend of me. "You always have to clean up?" she asked. "Seems like scut work to me."

At other moments she twitched her arm to threaten me, and make me stay right where I was.

There was nothing I could do but wait.

Our guest rigger finally returned from his walk. The doors slid open and gusted cold air in.

He came straight to the nook where we had the buffet. He often arrived right after I cleaned up, and then would scowl at me until I came back out with some food for him.

The stranger stood against the opposite wall, waiting. As the rigger looked at the empty buffet with disgust, his 'friend' stepped forward, and in an overly bold voice shouted "Villem!"

The rigger spun around. Then his arms drooped to his side and his face twitched when he saw her. He suddenly looked like an old man. His posture slumped, and the large coat seemed to weigh him down.

"You remember an old shipmate?" the stranger asked in a wheedling tone.

"Your handle was Black Dog. Though that's not what some called you. Yes, I remember you," Villem said evenly. "So you found me. What now?"

"Just want to talk, oh captain my captain," the stranger said. "Catch up on old business. Of the unfinished sort, yeah?"

"Let the girl go," the rigger said, nodding at me.

"To call Sargasso Security on us?" The stranger shook her head. "I don't need more of a record, captain. She'll stay put. You and I can talk without her overhearing well enough."

They switched to another language. It was a metallic language, with a chirps and strings of fluid consonants, punctuated only by sudden strings of swearing from both of them that made me jump.

This was not a friendly conversation. There was something not far from a snarl on our guest's lips, and the stranger grew more and more furious with each exchange.

The conversation ended with three of the spider drones clambered around the edge of the stairs. They leapt into the room with an explosion of angular limbs and speed, throwing themselves across the floor to get at the stranger.

"Damn it, Vill..." she shouted.

She shot her gun. The loud crack made me jump, and one of the drones exploded, ripped apart by the bullet. She fended off the two other drones as they fought to rip her gun and hand apart.

I scrambled across the floor on my hands and knees, eyes crazy wide and terrified, and hid behind the bar.

And then... I peeked out around the corner. I couldn't help myself. I had to know what the hell was going on. Our rigger had suddenly become *interesting* again.

Villem stood still, concentrating so hard he quivered. He was controlling the drones from deep inside his own head. Ordering them to attack, and to jump away from her shots.

Then he stepped forward himself, ducking low, and the drones moved in synch with him. They moved to disable the stranger as he stepped forward in an explosion of speed and movement matched to each drone's movement.

The three of them fought in a strange ballet of super-fast movement as she writhed about, trying to keep hold of her weapon.

Another drone died in an electrical-sparking fury of destruction, and then the last one ripped the gun in half with a last gasp of energy before it too died, riddled with more shots through its carapace.

The stranger pulled her mechanical hand free of the gun's shattered pieces. As she did so the hand changed itself into a long blade, rippling and moving into the new shape. She slashed at Villem, forcing him to take a step back, and then ran out the door leaving a trail of her blood behind.

Villem stumbled backwards, watching her run away. He pulled out a handful of blue cylinders, hands shaking as he tried to use them. But he slumped to the floor before he could, the injectors tumbling onto the carpet.

I ran out and kneeled next to him, ready to make the emergency call again, sure he'd been shot. And maybe a little piece of me was hoping he would end up in the hospital and out of the Inn. Mysterious and exciting. I'd hoped for that. But it had turned into people shooting guns in the Inn.

That was too much, I realized, my hands shaking.

I could have died, though adrenaline had kept me from even realizing it as they'd fought in front of me.

Villem grabbed my arm. "Pass the injectors over," he hissed. His hand shook so hard it felt like he would tear my arm out of its socket.

"You don't need drugs right now," I told him. What was he thinking?

"I need to *slow down*." Sweat rolled off his face. "I had to speed myself up to run the drones, to fight her. I'm overheating, Jane. Get me an injector before I damage myself any further, damn it. Now!"

I could hear him hyperventilating as I crawled around to pick up the injectors. I was so shaken by everything that had just happened I kept dropping them. My hands just wouldn't stop shaking.

When I finally handed him one he snatched it away and jammed it hard against his neck to trigger it. He began to relax after the hiss.

Sadayya swore from the stairs, then recovered and demanded: "What happened?"

She looked horrified, her hands flying to her mouth both to try and pull back the swearing and, I knew, in shock at what she saw. Chairs lay upended everywhere and dead spider drones sparked and writhed in place.

Villem lay on the floor. Blood spattered the carpet.

"Jane?" Sadayya shouted. "Are you okay?"

I nodded numbly. "He's hurt. I think he might be shot. I don't know."

Sadayya had to grab me first and look me over, just to make sure I was okay. After that, she crumpled a little and hugged me tightly to her, looking tired and scared.

The rigger lay on our floor, still breathing rapidly. He didn't respond to us as we waved our hands over his face. We couldn't see his eyes behind those black patches welded to his face, so we couldn't tell if he was conscious.

"Do we call Security?" I asked, looking around at the mess.

Sadayya took a deep breath. "We'll get written up. It'll be on the Inn's public record that this happened here. What will future guests think?"

She shook her head. I could tell she hated thinking that way. Thinking about business. It felt wrong to be thinking like that right now. But I realized she made sense.

"But what about Villem?" I asked. He might be hurt. Or worse.

"Who?"

I pointed at the rigger.

"I'll call Dr. Armstrong. He'll help," Sadayya said.

***

Dr. Armstrong came right away with a small black case that contained his tools and a built-in diagnostics computer that I'd seen often enough. He opened it and pulled out a blue, semicircle-shaped wand, like a hula-hoop cut in half. It clacked as he waved it over the rigger's body.

A three dimensional image appeared on the inside of the case's lid as Dr. Armstrong moved the wand around, giving us all a look at the rapidly beating heart of the rigger. There were several square boxes embedded in the man's ribs near the heart. And several small pumps located around the heart, ready to take over for it if it failed. Rigger upgrades.

Next up the doctor moved the wand over the rigger's head, and a secondary screen appeared, showing hundreds of little squiggles. Brain activity.

Dr. Armstrong rolled up the rigger's shirt sleeves, exposing a number of tattoos. "For the luck." "Mind the line!" and the last, a series of curvy lines and dots.

Dr. Armstrong peered at that last one more closely. "That's his resume," he said. "It's a type of code. Villem Osteonidus is his name, and those are the ships he has served, and the positions he's held. If you scan the code, the information will unpack and tell you an entire life story. If you have the right encryption key. All I can access is his name."

I stared at the wavy lines and wondered what was embedded in them.

Dr. Armstrong continued. "Spacers have their metabolisms accelerated to support superfast mind-states so they can serve the ships, and this man has burned himself out over his many years. He can't keep slowing down with those drugs and speeding up when he needs to. He'll drop dead of it. And he doesn't have much left in him."

He pressed a few buttons on a large injector of his own, selecting one of his hundreds of medicines compressed and held inside, and then injected Villem in the side of the neck.

"Villem? Can you hear us?" The doctor glanced at his readouts.

The rigger twitched. "That. Is not my name," he said.

Dr. Armstrong looked up at us and raised an eyebrow.

"He's lying," I whispered.

Dr. Armstrong shrugged. "We're going to move you

upstairs. Can you help us walk?"

"Yah," the rigger nodded slowly. "I can do that."

After we closed the door and left the man in his own bed, Dr. Armstrong gathered Sadayya and me together in the small hallway. "I have two pieces of advice: one, you need to get that man out of your inn. Two, do not tell Tia what happened. She does not need the stress, or the worry. You understand me?"

Sadayya nodded. So did I.

"I'm going to go check on her," Dr. Armstrong said.

"This rigger," Sadayya muttered, hugging me again close to her. "He will be the death of us."

Chapter Four

Villem recovered enough by lunch the next day to call for room service. But he ignored the sandwich I reluctantly delivered, waving it away. He lay on top of the covers of his bed, right where we'd left him.

"Jane… I need your help." He pushed himself up onto an arm. "I've been running myself fast all day, trying to track down anyone who might be here looking for me. I've been trying to get into the city's immigration databases. I'm exhausted now."

"You should eat, and rest. Armstrong said you needed rest," I told him.

I didn't want to help him anymore. I wanted him out of the Inn.

"I can rest when I'm dead," he hissed at me, struggling to sit up. His hands shook and sweat dripped from his chin. "And that'll be soon enough if you don't help me."

"What do you need?" I asked.

"In the bathroom, taped to the back of the mirror."

"I'm not going to be your enabler," I told him with a sigh. "You want to use those drugs, find someone else."

"Now that's a low thing to say," Villem said softly. "And right when I can barely get off this bed. Look, I know I got too amped up, burned too deep. I got carried away, but can you blame me? I almost died last night."

"Doctor Armstrong said you'll kill yourself if you keep doing this…"

"The doctor? I'm hardly flesh and bone. Jane, I'm as much a machine as I am a man, and what does *Doctor* Armstrong know of *machines*? Has he created something like me, able to spread his consciousness out through a network like I can? Able to speed up thought itself? What the hell does he know about those things? Men like me've been managing our

systems a lot longer than he has. I've lived through this
maelstrom long enough. I know my path. I know it's been
rough. I *know* I'm rough around the edges. But I know how far
I can take it."

He looked at me with those fused black windows over
his eyes.

I wavered. He had created himself, after all, hadn't he? It
made sense that he would know his own limits.

Villem changed direction. "Your mother is in the rough
herself, isn't she? I'll make you a bargain, Jane. Get me what I
need, and I'll pay six month's rent. Your family needs the
money. You have no guests in this little bed and breakfast of
yours. I promise you, I'll be dead, murdered, evicted or in the
hospital before the week is out."

I swallowed. He was right. I could take offense at the
bribe, but seeing the sallowness in his face, the raw fear, it
made me want to help. Both him and Sadayya. Sadayya was lost
in her own world of worries: I needed to pitch in where I
could. Just like I'd always helped around the Inn by cleaning
rooms, cooking, even registering guests.

I complained about it. I hated working at the Inn. More
because it felt like a future I would be trapped in for the rest of
my life. But no matter how much I hated it, I wasn't going to
turn my back on my own family.

"Send the money to the Inn's account," I said with
gritted teeth.

He licked his cracked lips and moved his fingers in the
air, typing details into an interface that only he could see. Then
he nodded. "It's done."

I used a dumb screen that was on the wall for guests...
and people like me without any machine implants. Villem had
sent the money to the Inn's account. It would help us scrape by
another month. "Okay."

The sink was festooned with bottles of skin creams and
pill bottles, which I ignored as I opened the cabinet to retrieve
several blue injectors.

Villem grabbed them eagerly from me and jammed one

into his neck.

"Oh, that's it," he said, melting back into his bed. "That's just definitely it. That woman, who came for me?"

"The Black Dog?"

"That's her handle, yes. You be careful of her. You see her again, you call Security. You run. They're here for my secrets." He laughed and looked over at the massive black slab of a trunk in the corner of his room. It hummed and hissed away. "I imagine all of Flint's crew is out here, looking for me. Those are dangerous people, that take up with Flint. Very dangerous. But I tell you, as long as they don't get the black spot into me, then there's still a fight left."

"The black spot?" I asked.

He was all but rambling now, everything coming out in a constant flow of words. It was hard for me to follow, and I cared less than I would have when I first met him. He wasn't interesting and exciting anymore. I saw him now as a scared, burned out old man with a dangerous past.

"They'll infect me with it. It'll take over my implants and force me to their summons, like a marionette jerked by its strings. I'd be compelled to walk right on over to them, yeah, give them what they want. You warn me, Jane. They still have to try and touch me. So you warn me if you see them, and I'll share everything with you. I'm an old man, with no one else in all the worlds. I'll give you points on the package, a piece of the cut, if you do good by me. I swear it. I'll give you a contract, if you save me from them. You'll be richer than you can imagine. Just don't call Security on me. Oh, I'll bet they'd love to see what I got hidden away here. You keep them all off me, you wouldn't believe the things I'll share with you. I swear it..."

His voice grew weaker and faded away, and after a long moment I realized he'd fallen asleep. Or passed out.

I creeped over to the bed, reaching out to him as if he were a dead mummy, and checked his pulse with a finger. His skin was clammy and, the moment I felt the twitch of his heart, I pulled my fingers away.

Outside, in the corridor, I couldn't decide what I should

do. Tell Sadayya that our guest had mysterious secrets that Security would be interested in? Or just call Security myself? Maybe Dr. Armstrong would know what to do?

I mulled my options over. But it all fled my mind when I saw Sadayya standing at the end of the hallway by the stairs waiting for me, her face torn with grief.

She didn't have to tell me what had happened: I knew that my mother Tia had died.

We'd known that it was coming. It had been a brewing thundercloud descending slowly upon our house for so long that I had gotten used to dealing with it day after day. And now the storm collapsed in the form of neighbors blowing in from the streets to coalesce around us with concern, food, and a flurry of hushed whispers.

I wasn't sure how I was expected to react. Because mostly I just felt empty inside. Hollow and tired, focusing on each step of what I had to do to get through it.

But out of all those different feelings that crept through me, the one I fought and hated, yet secretly welcomed, was the one of relief. Tia had struggled for so long, how was it fair of me to demand that she suffer longer just to leave things as they were?

With all of this on my mind, I didn't think about Villem for almost a full day. Not until the night of the wake.

Everyone crammed into the lobby, where someone had thoughtfully set up a projected image of Tia smiling on a beach somewhere in the Arabian Gulf where she and Sadayya first met. Next to that, a series of random scenes of our family played out.

Those happy people seemed like aliens to me at that moment.

But as empty inside as I felt, as numbed as I was, nothing shocked me more than the sight of Villem as he stumbled down the stairs in the middle of the wake. He could barely talk as he tottered his way around people, and then he fell to his hands and knees.

"Get him out of here," I begged the nearest neighbors.

This was all devastating enough as it was without a drugged rigger crashing through our grief. "Take him back upstairs."

Villem heard my voice. He looked over, not understanding what he'd done. "Just paying respec' to the captain of the house," he said, trying to brush people away.

Then he threw up on the floor.

I should have exploded with rage. But the truth was I felt disgusted and saddened.

I didn't have the energy to focus on his antics.

I turned my back to him as he was dragged up the stairs. An utter ass. A broken drug addict. Not worth my attention.

Chapter Five

Villem tried talking to me when I delivered food to his room the next day, but I was walking through a haze of my own sadness and didn't bother to listen to him. I felt like the depths of my brain had been depth charged. He might have been half machine, but the death of one of my mothers left me far more robotic than Villem could ever dream of being.

But he refused to let me retreat from his room. He hobbled up to his feet and hopped over until he blocked me from just running out of the door. "Jane, I really am sorry."

"Sorry doesn't change anything," I snapped, pushing him aside. His arms were still cold, clammy, and stick-like. The man was a scarecrow of a human being. "Everyone's *sorry*. But my mother is still dead. You still ruined the wake. And I don't get any of that back. You understand?"

He sat down on his desk chair with a shaky sigh. "It will never hurt less," he said softly.

"What?"

"That empty feeling in you right now. The hole. The missing bit. People aren't just things outside of you, they reach in and add something to you. When they die, it's ripped away, and there's a void left behind. They tell you time makes it easier. But that isn't true. When you think about them, realize they're gone, the pain is still there. I still miss all my friends who died on ships out there."

I myself looked like Villem right then: pale and trembling. Barely able to stand. "That isn't helping," I said in a small voice. My eyes had started to redden.

"Eventually, you get better at forgetting," Villem rasped quickly. "All the other things that overwhelm your mind fill in those gaps. And then you have to work at remembering that pain, that hole. And in some cases, that makes it worse. Not that time made it easier, but that time just... erases most of it. All your mates, your lovers, your kin, they become dust in the wind, no matter how tight you try to grab hold them."

I leaned against a wall, hardly able to find the energy to stand. "Why are you being so cruel to me?"

"Sweetheart, I'm not being cruel at all." Villem closed his eyes. "I'm telling you the things no one else does. Because they shower you with bullshit to keep you happy and protected. But I've seen too much, and I am not here to shelter or protect people's egos. Yours included. I call it as I see it. Because I see you, Jane. I know where you are. You're hungry. I can smell it on your sweat. You're hungry for more than just this inn. And I want to help you."

I thought he was just covering for his rude behavior again. I couldn't believe him. "You think you're doing a service to everyone. But you're really just a cruel, bitter, burned out old man, rationalizing your behavior."

Villem leaned forward, a gleam in his eyes. "Is that it? Is that all I am? Then why are you eager to spend so much time around me, Jane?"

He stood up, walked over to me, and I didn't like the look in his eyes. Calculating, scheming, and scary intense.

"If you come any nearer, I'll shout for the Inn to call Security," I warned.

Villem stopped. "I want to show you something."

He shuffled back to the large trunk and opened a section of it. Mist roiled in the air and blue light spilled out from the depths.

I stepped forward for a better look inside.

Villem pulled out a metal glove that trailed cables and tubes back into the trunk's depths.

"I told you I could manage my systems better than Doctor Armstrong. I have a basic rigger's medical kit in here. Among other things." He fitted the glove to his hand. It hummed as he flexed it, then made a fist. "You don't have any implants, do you Jane? You're naked to the digital world out there."

34

I stared daggers back at him. But he was right. I was like a blind child out in the world. And I had wanted nothing more than to change it.

"Sadayya wants me to experience the world as it is," I said, numbly repeating what I'd been told often enough when I argued with her. But I couldn't quite sell it to Villem as if it were my own belief. "She doesn't believe we should alter our bodies with implants. She will not give me permission. For now."

"And how long will 'for now' keep being?" he asked knowingly.

"I don't know." My voice broke slightly. "My... Tia had implants. But I don't think Sadayya will let me get neural implants until I'm old enough to do it legally without her permission."

Tia would have let me do it, I thought. I teared up again and hated myself for the wetness.

Villem reached forward with the glove. "If you want to see the hidden world around you, I can turn it on. And the implants will help you cope... in other ways. Trust me. The ability to better control your neurological swings can be added to the software."

I shook my head. Why was he tempting me with this now, of all times? How inappropriate. Who offered to do this sort of thing?

Drug-using riggers who didn't give a damn about any rules, who lived out in the dark vacuum far above the blue of the atmosphere, I thought. That's who.

I should walk out of the room, I knew. Walk out and just tell Sadayya.

And yet, I was still standing in front of him. "Sadayya will kill me."

"You were saving and planning to do it anyway." Villem crouched beside the trunk, staring up at me. "It takes two minutes, and then you'll be able to talk to the Inn without moving your lips. Control machines and access information with a thought. Come on. I know this is a bad time, and you feel guilty thinking about leaving. But you don't want to get trapped. And if you ever want to get out, you'll need this."

Hesitantly, I stepped over and squatted next to him. I shouldn't be doing this, I thought. Shouldn't even discuss it further with him. "I know I can't ever leave the Inn if I can't keep up with everyone else," I said. "It's something I'm going to *have* to do."

So why not do it now?

I'd rationalized a long time ago why I was going to sneak out and get implants before I was old enough to do it, and do it without Sadayya's permission.

"And if I have to do it at some point, does it matter when?" I said, as much to myself as to Villem.

"You're right," Villem said, and grabbed the back of my neck under my dreadlocks with his glove.

"Are you ready for this?" he asked.

No.

Yes.

I bit my lip. "Do it."

Pain shot down my spine as something injected itself in the base of my neck, and the entire room seemed to flex and glow with an orange light.

Villem puttered around, chittering at himself like a tiny animal. It all felt very distant to me. I tried to move my hands, but they remained at my side, as if suddenly turned to lead. I couldn't move anything.

I wanted to panic, but I couldn't muster up the energy for it.

"Can you hear me?" Villem boomed. His voice, no longer raspy and tired, brimmed with authority and dripped with a sense of leadership.

I tried to move my lips to answer, but nothing came out.

"Don't try to use your voice, just answer me."

Yes, I tried to scream.

"Easy does it, Jane. No need to shout. Loud and clear."

I'm talking to you?

"Nifty, eh? Now, Jane, I want you to open your eyes."

But they are open, I said. Or at least I thought I did.
Would he be able to hear all my thoughts?

I panicked again for a second.

"No Jane: OPEN THEM."

It felt like he slapped the back of my head with the metal
glove. My vision blurred, and then a waterfall of random
numbers and oddly shaped glyphs sluiced into the room and
thundered out the door.

Help!

Villem let go of me and I fell forward, catching myself
before I lost my balance. I was back in control and could move.

I looked around. The waterfall of figures had faded away.
But there was a ghostly outline in the room. As I looked at
different items, tiny bits of information popped up over them.
Just like when I used a screen, or information glasses.

The coffee pot needed attention and glowed a soft
orange, it had been twenty four hours since its last cleaning.
The carpets had a notice etched into them about the need for a
full antibiotic cleaning service. The mini-fridge, when I focused
on it, faded into transparency and showed its contents to me.

"You're a tinkerer, Jane. A smart one. This is your
birthright," Villem said, but it was his raspy, broken, real voice.
Not the one he'd transmitted directly into my head earlier.

He took the glove off and packed it back away into the
trunk, nestled beside capsules and more gleaming equipment.

"Come back when you have time and I'll teach you to use
it," he said. "I can't take back what I did to you at the wake.
But I can give you this gift, at least. It's the best I can do."

Chapter Six

I stood behind the small registration desk in the lobby by myself, staring off into nothingness.

Or that is what it looked like from the outside.

Okay, Jane, said Villem inside my head. His words came slowly, and somewhat fuzzily. When I'd last seen him he'd just been lying in his bed, too drugged to get up and move around. *Tell the carpet cleaner to begin.*

He was still committed to helping me, in his own strange way. And it beat standing in the lobby thinking about what I should have been thinking about or mulling over. Or wondering why for the last few nights I'd been up all night with the worst muscle cramps when they weren't due for at least a week yet.

I stared at the carpet cleaner, a round tub of a machine with bristles and a large reservoir of blue cleaner on top that sloshed gently back and forth.

I'd always hated having to walk up to it, pushing buttons to get it to start up. Or even worse, pushing it around the carpet manually. Sadayya said it built character. I said that was just something people said to get you to do pointless work a machine should actually be doing.

Focus, Villem told me from his room. *And don't try to force it.*

"Which is it?" I muttered. "Focus, or let it happen?"

I heard that, he said.

It was hard to talk to him, inside my own head, and try to use the carpet cleaner at the same time.

Here's the laundry machine, he said, and I blinked and wobbled as my head twisted inside out. I was seeing the lobby and the insides of the washing machine at the same time. Damp clothes had come to a stop.

The carpet cleaner began to run away from me, headed

for the wall.

Shit, I thought.

And then I shut my eyes and threw my hands out to the side, because it felt like I was falling over. The whole Inn spun around me.

I can't do this, I silently shouted at Villem. *Just everything stop!* Guilt hit me. And then a desire to run away from it. To focus on anything else.

Which is what I'd been doing all week, thanks to Villem. Keeping distracted.

It's a part of growing up, using implants, Villem said. *Everyone learns it, you will too. Stop whining. Now visualize a connection between you and the cleaner…*

I sighed and muted him without even thinking about it. I opened my eyes and saw that the cleaner sat still, a foot away from the wall.

Well, I'd done that at least.

Focus, but don't think too hard about it.

Maybe the washed up old man knew what he was talking about, I thought.

I blinked, realizing that someone was watching me from the corner of the desk. He'd walked in while I was closing my eyes, trying to control the machines and talk to Villem at the same time.

Like Villem, he had black metal patches fused over his eye sockets. He hunched over, as if used only to cramped, small spaces, but there may have been something wrong with his spine, too. He had no teeth, just a solid chrome band under his lips, and his exposed skin was blistered and chafed around the edges of the silk robes he wore.

"Hello," he said, and before I could reply he grabbed my arm and shoved a long walking stick hard into my ribs. "This is not a walking stick, but a railgun. You make a sound, and I'll shoot you and leave you for dead right here."

A hundred horrible thoughts ripped right through my imagination about what he wanted.

Villem, I shouted. But there was nothing. A deadness

hung in the air around us. I could feel it through the prickle in the back of my neck. The connectedness I'd just finally achieved had been smothered by a blanket of nothingness.

"Tell me what room he's in," the man said.

"Who?" I asked.

The man twisted my arm and slammed it into the wooden desk so hard I screamed. "You know who I'm talking about. Don't play games. The rigger, little girl."

"Little girl?" I was momentarily offended and tried to stand up straight in outrage. But he twisted my arm again in that completely firm grip. I swore and bit back tears.

"Take me to him, now." The voice did not sound like it had much patience left. He punctuated the order with a stab of the walking stick.

"What are you going to do to him? Kill him?" I asked as he forced me toward the stairs. He jammed my hands up behind my back, almost to the edge of dislocation. My shoulder blade screamed.

"Kill him? No, no, that's not what I have in mind. I just want to talk to that murderous thief. You take me up to his room, and knock on the door. Tell him he has a delivery."

I should have been terrified, but I think I'd been numb for so long that week it left me anesthetized to my own emotions. I walked slowly up the stairs, screaming for help via my newfound powers, but all that happened were error messages and weird pop-ups in my vision that all indicated something was wrong.

This man could jam implants.

When we got to Villem's room I tentatively knocked at the door.

It took a few minutes for anything to happen. I'd known Villem was doped up. But he still managed to eventually shuffle to the door. When it opened the man shoved me forward into the room and stepped in after me.

Villem gurgled horribly and stumbled back for his bed. He tried to grab for something under his pillow.

The man raised his walking stick. It hissed and jerked in

40

his hands, and the air in front of it zapped and wavered. The pillow disappeared in an explosion of down and fabric.

A fist-sized hole in the bed sizzled and spat.

And behind it, a same-sized hole in the wall glowed red.

"Now, Villy, I wouldn't do that," said the man behind me. "I've got my old railgun here, and I'll just as happily shoot you instead of doing what needs done next. You know I have the better reflexes and targeting wetware. So you just sit right there while I do what needs done. Girl, step forward and grab his wrist, and then pull him over here. But slowly."

I shakily did as I was ordered.

The new rigger reached out with what looked like a piece of paper that he slapped into Villem's palm. Villem grunted and rolled his hand into a fist, looking utterly defeated.

"Well, that wasn't so hard now, was it, Villy?"

Villem opened his mouth to answer, and the man behind me leapt away. We listened, both stock still, as his boots click-clacked their way down the stairs with surprising speed.

That dead feeling in the air disappeared with him.

"What the *hell*, Villem?" I shouted. "I'm calling Security. You have to leave the Inn. You can't do this to us anymore. You just can't!"

Even with the gift of implants, he had to go. They weren't worth dying over. Villem certainly wasn't.

Villem held up an arm as if trying to block my sudden anger. "I can *fight it*," he said with intensity. "I've been working on a way to fight it. Don't worry, Jane. You'll still get your fair share. I won't cut you out."

"What are you talking about?" I asked. "You crazy old piece of crap, what *the hell* are you even talking about?"

This was the last straw. We needed to kick him out. Him and his dangerous, strange 'friends' and his drugs and his moody tirades and everything to do with him.

Sadayya and I needed a fresh start. We couldn't be dragged down with him.

Even though Villem was just sitting on the edge of his bed now, his entire body started to tense, like he was a weightlifter trying to raise hundreds of pounds into the air. I could see every single strand of muscle under that papery skin strain.

"You'll never have to work again, Jane! I promise. You'll be richer than you can imagine." Villem croaked this out and slid over, balling himself up into a fetal position.

He struggled to raise his hand, struggled as if it were made out of lead. There was a black mark swirling around his wrist where the other man had touched it. Like a living tattoo.

Villem was fighting it with every piece of power he had left. Because the mark, even as it tried to sink itself into his skin, quivered and threw itself against some kind of barrier. That was why Villem had curled up, why he could barely breath. He was trying to stop the tattoo from burrowing further into his skin.

"I. Can. Refuse." He stammered this out in a wild scream, scrabbling at the black caps over his eyes with his other hand.

I stared in horror as he pulled them away, surgical staples tearing free of flesh and blood dripping from around his milky white eyes.

Villem's frosted eyes stared right through me as he fought whatever invisible thing the dot was doing to him. I heard something pop inside him, and a leg jerked, as if someone other than Villem controlled it.

He stumbled out of his bed, yanked free of it as if pulled by ropes. He screamed in defiance as he crawled on his hands and knees to the door where I stood. But Villem regained control, frothing spit as he continued his rabid yowl, and managed to freeze on the floor.

I heard his joints crack, and one of his arms break, from the strain of muscle fighting muscle.

Villem bore down so hard his eyes bloomed red from burst blood vessels. Still on hands and knees, his entire body quivered and spasmed, and then he slumped into stillness at my feet.

"I beat it," he whispered with a faint grin. "We'll be rich,

Jane, you and I. We'll get to the trove... just take this... you must, hold it for me..." a black pebble rolled out of his fingers onto the carpet and bumped against my feet, where it glowed briefly.

When Villem said those last words, it was with a long trickle of blood that leaked from the corners of his lips. And then the frostiness over his eyes clouded over further as they rolled back into his head.

He died right there on the carpet as I watched, the black spot still spinning slowly on his wrist.

It was too much. My mother, now this broken, mad man lying on the carpet in front of me. When Sadayya found me, I was curled up against the wall near the bed screaming with rage-filled tears.

Not as much for Villem, but because of everything.

Just... everything.

Chapter Seven

Sadayya dropped to her knees and wrapped me in a tight hug the moment she ran into the room after hearing the screams.

"It's over now." Sadayya said in between deep breaths. "He finally killed himself. Drugged himself into oblivion. It's okay."

"But he didn't." I carefully pushed at his arm with a shoe to show her the black spot. "He was infected with some kind of software. He died trying to fight it off."

"Don't touch it," Sadayya hissed, startled and scared.

"We should call Security," I said.

She nodded, and we wiped tears from our eyes and steadied ourselves with each other. It was over.

It was over.

And right at that moment the doors to the back of the Inn exploded.

At least, that's what it sounded like from upstairs.

"They must be coming for Villem," I said. "They tried to use that black spot thing on his hand to force him to do what they wanted." He had died fighting it. Now they were coming for him.

"Forcible intrusion alert," the Inn announced loudly. "Alerting Sargasso Secu…" The Inn's security software cut off mid word.

Whoever was downstairs had hacked the Inn and shut it down. And quickly.

This was bad. So bad.

We ran out of the room. But not before I grabbed the black pebble off the carpet and slid it into my pocket. If we got questioned by security, I thought, they might want to take a look at it.

I certainly didn't want them thinking I'd made anything up.

Outside, in the hallway, we ran for the stairs. But a voice from around the corner and down the stairs stopped us cold. "Come out, Villy-boy. Don't hole up waiting for us, because we'll come in shooting and take what we're here for from you. Better to stop fighting the black spot and just walk on down."

Sadayya and I looked at each other. The jamming of the Inn distracted me, because everywhere I looked random objects popped up in the air and burst and fizzled away. I was seeing things via my neural taps that were randomly generated by whatever was erasing all the normal information that hung in the air.

It was distracting and scary.

The voice continued. "We swear, one mate to another, we'll leave you with your life if you walk on down."

We ran back from the stairs down the hallway to the emergency exit by the window at the end, but we saw the railings quivering outside the window. Someone was loudly clumping their way up the metal stairs toward us.

Trapped halfway down the hall, we froze. Sadayya didn't seem to know what to do. She was acting like she was stuck in honey, looking slowly around herself in a delayed panic.

I grabbed her by the arm and pulled her toward the nearest room door.

Open, I commanded as I ran forward. I slammed into a dead door. My shoulder throbbed.

That's right, the Inn had been hacked and shut down. These new tricks I'd learned didn't work.

I quickly fumbled around for Sadayya's master ID card. All the locks had independent backups.

We had seconds.

The room door opened just as the window to the emergency exit shattered. Someone jumped through it into the hallway as I quietly, gently, with a wince at the slight sound of the lock clicking, shut the door behind us.

We stood in the room right next door to Villem Osteonidus's room.

Sadayya opened her mouth to say something. But these

were riggers. About to attack. They would be amped and keyed up. No doubt they'd be able to hear almost anything.

I clamped my hand over my mother's mouth and shook my head.

Then I lead her into the bathroom and closed the door as much as I dared. It was cold in here. I was shaking from the chills.

I pointed at the bathroom tub, a finger on my lips. Sadayya understood and got in. I crawled in after her and drew the shower curtain shut.

We faced each other, both terrified, and waited.

Chapter Eight

The men who'd invaded the Inn remained convinced for several minutes that they were in the middle of full on, and rather tense, standoff.

I recognized the voice of the man who'd forced me to deliver the black spot. "Villy," he bellowed. "Goddamnit, get down here. It doesn't have to end like this."

The other men just outside our door shouted for a full minute, making Sadayya and me twitch with each threat. Then they switched to wheedling promises. They rotated between threats and begging Villem to show his face for a full minute, everyone shouting over each other.

Then someone said "Forget it. We've given him his chance."

A shotgun round was chambered. I shivered as I recognized the unique clacking and pumping sound.

By unspoken agreement the men in the Inn opened fire into the room next door. Sadayya and I grabbed each other hard. We may even have whimpered, but over the roar of gunfire no one heard us.

The moment the shattering sounds stopped, I heard the crack of Villem's door being kicked inward. Heavy boots clumped around in the room next to us.

"He's dead," someone announced.

"Obviously," came the snorted response. "He wasn't walking out after all that."

"No. I mean: he was dead already."

"It's not on him," said another disappointed voice.

And I heard that one familiar, snarling voice. "Then quit standing there and search the place! We don't have much time before someone shows up."

"Sargasso Security just got the phone call about gunshots fired," one of the intruders reported. "ETA five minutes before this place is swarming with Inspectors."

"Then *move* people! Let's get this and get out. Let's go let's go let's go."

I listened to the crack of furniture flipped and torn apart. Glass broken. More thumping around and a lot of very creative swearing involving people's mothers and orifices.

"Nothing in his trunk. Nothing in his accounts. He's got a few hundred thousand just sitting around in investments we can take," an intruder standing close to the other side of the bathroom wall from us reported.

"Damn you, you know we're not here for that." Something smashed against the wall just above our heads, a corner puncturing through the walls.

It was the large slab of trunk. It had been thrown at the man, missed, and buried its end into the wall.

I didn't want to think about how dangerous someone was who could lift that entire thing and throw it against a wall in frustration.

"We need Flint's logs! Find the damn logs!"

"Ain't here."

"He has to be hiding them somewhere in the Inn. Start kicking in doors until you find it."

"Security's three minutes away."

"Dirk, shut up! Who cares about friggin' Security when the logbook has to be right here. None of you even had the balls to look Villem in the eye to give him the black spot, but I managed it. So do me a favor and try to man up a little. Once we have the logbook and are off Earth we're untouchable."

The intruders started kicking in doors. The slamming and splintering sounds started on the other side of the hallway. After each door got kicked in the rigger shouted back. "Nothing in here!"

"Nothing down here."

I turned and saw my mother's face. The blood had drained from it.

We were going to be found.

The door to our room shuddered once, struck by

something really, really big on the other side.

"You must be…" I whispered into Sadayya's ear as I moved to cover her in the tub, "…absolutely still."

On the second hit the door gave in.

I could feel my mother take a deep breath next to me. Too much movement, I thought. I activated the scarf with a thought, now, instead of physically having to turn it on, as the door to the bathroom opened and light spilled in.

Not a muscle could twitch. I could feel my elbow shoved against the hard plastic compound of the tub, the tickle of sweat down on my legs that wanted to quiver.

We're not here. Let the scarf do its technological magic, fooling the rigger's augmented eyes. Taking images of what was behind me and projecting that to him.

"Pew: Security's here," someone in the hallway announced.

The familiar voice in Villem's room swore, then said, "hold them down. John, Dirk, hold them down long enough for us to get out the windows. Basic running fire and retreat."

Whoever stood by our bathroom door left abruptly, running down the corridor.

I let out a deep breath and collapsed into my side of the tub.

"Take a position!" one of the intruders shouted. "Here they come."

The Inn erupted with gunfire again. The smack of bullets, and the cacophony of glass shards raining down onto the floors, kept us huddled inside the bathtub.

I heard the intruders leave through the windows, and a few seconds later two Sargasso Security Inspectors in full combat gear swept into our room.

"Hands up and identify yourselves!" they shouted.

"Please don't shoot! It's the Hawkins,'" we stammered as we blinked into the blinding bright lights and gun muzzles.

One of the Inspectors grabbed us by the arm and pulled us out. They lead us back down the stairs, where Sadayya and I looked around in a daze. Bullet holes pocked the walls everywhere, and framed pictures hung askew or broken. Pieces of glass glittered on every surface. The whole Inn had been turned into a battleground.

"We're ruined," Sadayya said, in shock, as we passed through it all.

The doors to the lobby lay on the ground, blasted out of their grooves. Security vehicles ringed the street, lights blinking away.

I focused, inward, trying to shove it all away and just think about myself. Where I stood. My place in the universe.

For a brief moment, everything around me dwindled away. The lights, the people, the sounds. Everything imploded inwards and faded away.

When I looked up, the sky had become a massive grid of information that I didn't understand.

Something was wrong with my vision. Some kind of rigger malfunction laying itself down over my senses. Probably due to my stress levels. And Villem's custom implants inserted into the back of my neck.

I breathed out again, and it all began to fade.

"What's wrong with her?" one of the Inspectors asked, pointing at me.

Everyone stepped back away from me.

Sadayya looked around. "What do you mean?" The dazed expression on her face faded. "What do you *mean?*"

I looked down at myself and saw it. Thanks to Villem's neural upgrades, I could see that traced out blue lines ran through my skin. Like an elaborate, whole body tattoo, the glowing electric blue ran just on top of my brown skin where ever I could see it. And a soft haze of blue sparkles surrounded the blue lines. In fact, because of them, I was glowing all over.

I stared at my blue, filigreed arms, not understanding.

"Get back from her," a woman ordered the Inspectors around me.

At my side, one of the Inspectors pulled out a handgun.

I recognized the woman loudly giving orders as Chief Inspector Isadora Duncan. I'd seen video of her giving a briefing about a murder case once. She had short, blond hair and a Chilean accent, and her lips were tight with anger.

"We have a level three bioware contamination possibility," she said, looking right at me. "At the very least: unlicensed bioware."

"Bioware?" Sadayya said, her voice cracking. "Implants?"

I looked over at her. I saw the anger and hurt on her face. More than just the Inn had been ruined tonight.

Chapter Nine

"You're running hot," a medic said quietly as he scanned me over in the back of an ambulance. I'd been hustled into the vehicle, the doors shut tight behind me, for all the world seeming like prison doors closing to me. "You shouldn't overclock your body like that without coolant upgrades. You'll fry your brain."

I stared at him. We both sat on the bench in the back as he used the ambulance's systems to study me. He had quite lovely blue eyes. And didn't quite make any sense.

"What?"

He frowned at me, and then changed expressions. Before he'd seemed a bit impressed. Now, annoyingly, he acted as if he were talking to a child.

"You know when you have a fever? If you get too high of a fever it cooks your brain. In this case, you have implants all around your skull, secondary processing units, and synaptic upgrades all throughout. When they're operating at peak, they give off too much heat. You'll cook yourself. And die."

I waved that aside. Of course I knew that. "That happens to riggers," I muttered. No one with normal implants dealt with that. Small units didn't dump enough heat to cause trouble.

"Sweetheart," he said in a patronizing, but rather earnest tone of voice. "You're dripping with advanced rigger neural technology. Some of it's so advanced it's not even licensed down here, planet-side. That's why you triggered that alarm."

"No, no," I said, seeing his mistake. "It's just a simple upgrade. So I can see consensus spaces out in public, and operate machinery. Just a simple communications overlay."

He shook his head. "It wasn't a simple upgrade. You've got crew-class nanotechnology floating around your system. Self-replicating DNA strands are rebuilding major parts of your body. You're a walking supercomputer, just like any rigger. And it's all cutting edge bioware computing, not chips. The chip in your neck was just the source. A small factory, if you will, pumping out the changes to the rest of you and coordinating the install cycle. Now, you're not infectious, the bioware just tripped our alarms. You're cleared. But you really do need to be careful when speeding up your reflexes and mental processes. Okay?"

I nodded, dazed, as he handed me a shoulder ice pack to wear. Then he had me drape another over the top of my head.

I thought back to the moment in the bathtub, where I was shivering away.

Then I remembered the moments right before we hid in that room. Where Sadayya had seemed to be moving and thinking so slowly.

She hadn't been moving slowly. Instead, I'd sped myself up, utilizing all this new... bioware that had been installed in me without my even realizing it.

Why had Villem done this to me?

I hated him with a supernova-sized explosion of furious, white-hot anger that I shut down as the ambulance door opened.

"Ms. Hawkins?" The Chief Inspector stood silhouetted in the bright lights that now lit up the exterior of our Inn. She motioned at me to come with her. "I want to show you something."

"I want to talk to my mother," I insisted. I needed to attempt damage control. To talk to her, even if she didn't want to hear it.

Chief Inspector Duncan glanced over at Sadayya's back, covered in a blanket as she sat on the sidewalk facing pointedly away from us. "She doesn't want to talk to you right now. Anyway, I need you to come with me."

***

On the other side of the ambulance three stretchers sat in a line.

"One my Inspectors died in the shoot-out," Chief Inspector Duncan said. "Do you know who those two riggers are in the stretchers? One was a guest of the Inn."

I swallowed and looked at the three bodies. Until Villem's death, I'd never seen a dead body in real life before. It was unsettling, now, to have the time to just stare at these.

They looked human, and yet not-human. Until I saw a dead body I never realized how animated we all were, even when at rest. Even unconscious, or in a deep sleep, the slow rise of a chest, the stir of an eye, the tension of muscles, all added up to a sense of vitality.

These were just human shapes. Utterly still. Unmoving. Unnerving.

There was Villem, of course. I told her everything I knew about him. And next to him, a man in Security uniform.

I looked at the third still body. "They called that man there 'Pew.' He was the one who attacked me. He forced me to give Villem that black spot thing."

"I see…" she froze and looked off to the right, listening to something being whispered to her by communications implants.

Chief Inspector Duncan grimaced.

"Our software is putting together some connections. Both 'Pew' and Villem Osteonidus turn out to have served as crew aboard the *SparkFlint*. Under different names, back then."

My jaw dropped.

Here I'd been living under the same roof as a man who'd seen history itself. A man who'd seen one of the most insane space wars to ever have been recorded.

A living sparship so intelligent it became deranged, turned back on its creators, and that had come within just a few lightyears of marauding through the Solar System itself.

Another inspector on the sidewalk swore. "Chief, *she's* conferencing in."

"I know," Chief Inspector Duncan snapped. "Everybody look sharp!"

A loud snap cracked the air, and the hologram of a

woman appeared next to us.

I gasped. "Lady Woodgrove!"

The Lady herself, in person, or as close as someone like me would ever get. I'd seen her face often enough, watching her travel around parts of the universe I would have done anything to get to: the gas clouds of Jupiter, the Martian tenements, or even off the double-stars of Centauri.

And further.

With the right implants, you didn't just see the sights, you could have the Lady Woodgrove's actual memories, taken by high-resolution brain scanners at the moment she saw these wonders, and have them added to your brain via a reverse scanning process.

People said they weren't perfect, it wasn't like reliving the event, more like a half-remembered dream, but it was a strong taste of the experience.

Lady Woodgrove owned Sargasso City. Or at least, most of it.

She was thin, but not skeletal. Strong biceps under her silver-gray shirt. Bright green eyes that made me feel like she was looking down at me, even though she was shorter than me. And such an angular face. It looked more rounded on the shows, but maybe that had been make up, I thought. Or digital processing.

"Bring all the evidence to my estate," Woodgrove said, looking around. "Except for the bodies."

"Yes ma'am," Chief Inspector Duncan said.

"Anything else you can tell me right now, Chief Duncan? What did they want from Mr. Osteonidus?"

At this point, I'd just been staring at her. Now I reached into my pocket and pulled out the black pebble. It was the first moment I'd had to show it to anyone. "I... I think I can help."

Everyone turned to stare at me, and I shrank back a little.

I preferred not being the center of everyone's attention. My style was more scarf and near-invisibility.

But I couldn't hold on to the pebble. Not when it had cost people's lives. Besides, I had no idea what it was, or if it was what everyone was looking for.

"Villem tried to give me this. I think it may be what they were looking for. I'm not sure, though."

Chief Inspector Duncan looked down at it, but did not reach for it.

"I need a tech," she said, after a small pause.

One of the inspectors ran over. "Chief?"

She pointed at the pebble. "What is that?"

The tech inspector pulled on a glove, picked it up, and looked at it through a monocle on her right eye that glittered as it lit up with information.

"Delivery mechanism. A biodrive of some sort. It triggered already."

Lady Woodgrove's eyebrows arched up with interest, but she didn't say anything.

"So we're out of luck?" Chief Inspector Duncan asked.

"Not so fast, Chief." The tech nodded at me. "Got some traces left on it, and they type-match to those signatures on Jane Hawkins here."

Now the chief sighed even louder. "Jane?"

"I don't know what you're talking about," I said, quite honestly.

"You walked out of the Inn glowing like neon sign," the tech said. "The information that was on this pebble was recognized and accepted by your biological signature. Whatever information that was on it, is in you now. Encoded and matched. *You're* the delivery mechanism now."

I screwed up my face in doubt. "This is *crazy*."

"Can you still see those sigils on your skin that you were projecting earlier?" the tech asked.

I looked down at my arms. The blue lines were there, just beneath my skin.

As I stared at them they glowed slightly brighter.

"I still see them," I said.

"If you flare them up bright enough, we'll be able to see them as well. Might be able to try decoding them—"

Lady Woodgrove interrupted. She was looking at me, and

I didn't quite know what to make of her expression. I felt like a small animal in front of a hungry predator. I wasn't sure whether to take off running, or stand still and hope that I wasn't being noticed, even though I know I had been.

"So then what those very dangerous men are *now* looking for, Jane Hawkins… is you," Lady Woodgrove said.

Chapter Ten

The Woodgrove estate sat on a section of Sargasso's edge. Most of the city's rim featured upscale condos and expensive ladder apartments that spilled over the edge and swayed as the city gently moved, like square tassels dangled over the ridge of a steel hat.

Instead of compact urban housing, the Woodgrove estate shimmered green with gardens and open air, something too expensive to experience in the rest of the crammed city.

I stared at the orange trees, banana trees, bushes, and the strangeness of the wasteful, unused and open idleness of the flat grass golf course as I was escorted into the estate by a full Sargasso Security team. All of this was at the Lady Woodgrove's request (or order, one didn't ignore a request by Lady Woodgrove).

A car drove us through the arches, then down into a tunnel into the back of the Woodgrove mansion.

Within minutes I stood inside of a private library the size of our entire Inn, filled with neck-craningly tall shelves packed with honest-to-goodness old books.

Floor-to-ceiling glass windows at the front of the library completed the stunning effect. The city was pushing through low-lying clouds as I entered. But within a minute the clouds passed by, and sunlight filled every nook and cranny of the giant library. Dust motes danced and sparkled in the sunbeams.

Half a mile below us, the tiny waves of the Atlantic frothed and broke in miniature.

Lady Woodgrove herself, live and in the flesh, waited at the corner of the library near a large, polished wooden desk with a brass lamp.

"Welcome to the estate, Jane," she said. "Though I'm very sorry it's under circumstances like this. On another day, I would have had someone take you on the full tour."

I stared around the library some more. And then asked, "where's Sadayya?"

"Your mother does not want to be a part of this conversation right now," said a familiar voice.

I turned around. "*Dr. Armstrong?*"

I hadn't realized how nervous I was about being alone in the library with Lady Woodgrove until he appeared. I sort of deflated a bit.

"You seem surprised," he said.

"You know Lady Woodgrove?"

He smiled. "When I was younger, I served as an emergency medical technician with one of her expeditions. I kept away from the cameras, I'm not a public sort of person. When they found out I was your family doctor, I was called in. Now, we need to talk about your upgrades, don't we?"

The focus was now back on me.

I swallowed.

"What we want is a DNA sample, Jane." Lady Woodgrove held up a cotton swab. "We'd like to use that to try and decode what was hidden with you."

That seemed reasonable enough. And this was *Lady freaking Woodgrove*, after all. I reached out and took the swab. "Okay."

I rubbed the inside of my cheek and handed it back.

"Thank you," Lady Woodgrove said, with a quick smile. And just like that, the sunlight of her attention shifted away from me.

She strode smoothly back over the heavy, polished marble floor to her desk, where she set the swab on a small square black plate.

It lit up with a green glow, and the swab slowly melted away.

The surface over the desk exploded with representations of spiral DNA.

My DNA.

For several minutes the spirals rotated through the air, blinking several times, then rotating to another piece. Each time a strand of my DNA rotated away, a sad bleep filled the air.

"Well," Dr. Armstrong muttered. "That is disappointing."

"What?" I asked.

"Lady Woodgrove just used most of the raw computing power laced throughout this entire city to try and crack the encryption hidden away now in your very cells," Dr. Armstrong said. "It's impossible."

The sad bleep filled the room again.

The Lady Woodgrove's lips were pressed tight together. "Not impossible, Doctor. But cracking the neural key that can unencode the information contained in her DNA, well, that would most likely kill Jane."

For just the briefest of moments, Lady Woodgrove looked disappointed.

Then she smiled grimly. "Well, Jane, you do not have to worry. We won't be stripping your brain out of your head, cell by cell, to solve this problem. But it is a shame we came this close. I would have liked to have known what those riggers were after. And what Mr. Osteonidus hid in you."

She sat down in the giant leather chair by her desk and looked glumly at the DNA spirals hanging over the desk, then waved at it irritably. The images all faded away.

"There will be other opportunities," Dr. Armstrong said, a faint thread of consolation in his manner.

"Not like this," Lady Woodgrove said. Her green eyes narrowed. "Not with *SparkFlint*'s old crew running around, trying to get their hands on this information. So damn close."

Dr. Armstrong spread his arms and looked at me with a grimace. "Forgive her callousness. She's been obsessed with the *SparkFlint* for a while, it's a long-standing hobby of hers." And then, in a warning sort of tone, aimed at Lady Woodgrove, he said, "It's not like Jane hasn't been through a lot today already."

Lady Woodgrove nodded. And then waved me away. Dr. Armstrong approached. In any second, I would be asked to leave. Dr. Armstrong would probably accompany me out of the mansion to bring me back home to my mother.

I didn't want to go.

I wanted to find out more.

Villem Osteonidus had turned the Inn upside down. He'd destroyed it. And he'd updated me with crazy-weird rigger technology. My body shimmered with virtual tattoos, and I could light myself up like one of those deep sea fish. I wanted to know why.

I *deserved* to know why.

"Why are you obsessed with the *SparkFlint*?" I asked quickly, stepping out to the side so I could see Lady Woodgrove again. "Wasn't it destroyed in the war?"

Dr. Armstrong sighed, just loudly enough for me to hear him. He didn't want me prodding Lady Woodgrove down this conversational path. "The *SparkFlint*..." he said in an annoyed manner, "...had the intelligence, speed, and raw computational power of a master artificial intelligence, fitted with the ability to fly between stars. But the damn ship was a thug."

"During the Kai Hanimar Conflict it was given free reign to armor itself up and get weaponized," Lady Woodgrove said, but in a gritty, lips curled up, sort of way. "It began boarding ships throughout demilitarized zones to 'inspect' them. After the conflict faded, it kept boarding ships, stealing cargo. The crew it retained: all hardened criminals and dangerous mercenaries. Within six months it built a criminal cartel that spanned lightyears. And by the end of the year, it had stolen more wealth in raw materials than you can imagine. Probably more than I can imagine. And I, Jane, can imagine quite a lot."

Dr. Armstrong jumped in again. "The *SparkFlint* hoarded exotic rare earth metals, among other things. Cached them away, somewhere in the depths of space. And the reason Lady Woodgrove is hunting it is that the *SparkFlint* boarded and destroyed several ships with major investments of her's aboard. That ship cost her. Dearly."

I thought about all that for a long moment. "So if you figured out the map from my DNA, what would you have done?"

"I would have commissioned a sparship," Lady

Woodgrove said. "Mortgaged a piece of the city for it. From Canaveral, and I have some very good contacts there, I would have headed out to find the trove. And I would have paid you one hell of a finder's fee, Jane."

"How much treasure do you think the *SparkFlint* hid?" I asked. "Realistically?"

Lady Woodgrove looked out of the windows thoughtfully. "Realistically? The entire gross national product of a large nation? More than any CEO or corporation or King of old."

That much.

I swallowed. Too freaking unreal. I steadied myself against the wooden desk. Not because of the money. But because of what I realized was going to happen because of it.

"Lady Woodgrove," I said.

They both looked at me. They heard that quaver in my voice. Realized I knew something more than I'd let on. Lady Woodgrove was eyeing me like a shark would stare at its kill. She stood up and stalked forward, looking right at me. I was in the brightness of her focus again. "Yes?"

"The *SparkFlint*'s old crew, they're never going to stop trying to find me to strip this information out. They're going to kill me." My hands shook.

Lady Woodgrove stepped over and put a hand on my shoulder. "We can get you guards…"

I cut her off, and moved her hand away. "For the rest of my life? They'll always be after me."

I thought back to the moment on the street, when I'd lit up. When everyone had noticed the rigger tech symbols glowing over my skin. I thought back to the information scrawling across the sky.

"I think…" I said, and took a deep breath.

Center yourself, I thought.

And this time, it was easier to go back inside myself.

What was it Villem told me? Focus, but not too muck. Let it happen.

I could sense the room, the shafts of sunbeams

crisscrossing the air.

The gentle hum of air through vents.

The thrum of the city's engines below my feet.

And then it all faded away, dwindling to that spot in the center of myself.

Everything balled itself up and rolled away, replaced with gridlines. Here I stood, above the ocean. Hanging in the air by myself.

Figures rained down from orbit, like a brief meteor shower, then settled into place like a violet curtain.

There was, in this new sky of mine, a new sun. A faint, distant beacon.

I reached for it and waved it closer.

It zoomed, an effect that rearranged all the other data in a way that made me queasy. A cluster of rocky bodies rushed at me, and I had to fight the urge not to throw my hands up in the air.

The rocks stopped, laid out in front of me.

And then a barrage of information unfolded. Walls of data. Manifests, and windows with pictures of vacuum-safe storage units and where they were located in the cluster.

I tapped on one.

"What are Oscillia Q-B storage units?" I asked out loud. "There are millions of them listed."

There had been a distant buzzing sound. Like a mosquito trying to say my name over and over again.

"Jane," it said again.

I let go of everything and snapped back into the room.

"I'm okay," I said, realizing that Dr. Armstrong had moved forward. "Did you see anything?"

Dr. Armstrong's jaw tightened. "We saw a lot of it, maybe not as much as you. But we saw the map, and the beacon. You lit this entire room up, Jane. It was hard to ignore."

Lady Woodgrove grabbed both my shoulders and looked right into my eyes, startling me. "To answer your question, Jane, Oscillia Q-B units are extremely valuable. More so than

63

any rare metals. My question now is, are you willing to go with us?"

"Go with you?"

"You are the map, Jane. You know that. And you can read the map, too."

I stared into those mega-famous green eyes like a small animal in headlights, frozen.

"I can't imagine not going," I said in a small voice. The tremor was back in it. Because I so badly, so desperately wanted to flee. The killers. My mom. Sargasso.

Memories.

Lady Woodgrove let go of my shoulders. Now she was all business. She had resumed her casual imperiousness once more, like a comfortable shawl. This was a lady used to absolute control and getting what she wanted. "I have to get to Canaveral, Armstrong. Take care of Jane and any details you need to on this end."

"There's just one thing I'm afraid of," Dr. Armstrong said.

"Yes?" Lady Woodgrove paused and raised an eyebrow.

"You."

"Me?"

"Yes, you. You're a public personality. A trillionare, famous throughout many worlds. Very... visible. There are people who follow your every move. And the *SparkFlint*'s crew is out there and hunting. You can't tip your hand about what we're doing at all. It'll put our lives in danger."

Lady Woodgrove ran her fingers through her hair and smiled. "Oh, I'll be a ninja about all this. Black ops and disguises all around. I promise."

She turned to sweep out of the room, but I raised a tentative hand. "There's... something you two haven't figured out yet."

"What's that?" Dr. Armstrong asked.

"We need my mother's permission for me to go."

"Oh, that." Woodgrove waved my objection away. "Yes, she did refuse to come down here for this little chat. She's really angry with you."

"Really angry would be an understatement," I said. "It's going to be apocalyptic back at the Inn."

Lady Woodgrove smiled. "I'll go talk to her, Jane, on your behalf... and mine. I'm sure she and I will come to an arrangement. I can be persuasive, and this is my city, after all, that she lives in. That usually counts for something. Your job is to get packed and prepared. We'll have a ship and crew by tomorrow. The faster we get off planet the better!"

Chapter Eleven

I packed quickly, making extra sure the invisibility scarf was tucked into the compartment at the top of my travel case. Outside my room, I could hear the buzz and clunking of construction drones putting the Inn back together. All at the Lady Woodgrove's personal expense.

From my porthole-shaped window I glimpsed security drones patrolling the air around the Inn. Several Inspectors walked around, looking at anyone on the street who got too close with a sort of professional scowl.

The floorboard right next to my doorway squeaked.

I picked up some color-variable spider-silk pants and a mechanic-black jacket.

"You made a deal with Lady Woodgrove," I said, without turning around. My implants told me who was standing at the door. It was Sadayya. "She pays off our debt and rebuilds the Inn. I go with her."

Simple. Rational. Everyone won.

I got what I wanted: escape. Lady Woodgrove got what she wanted: me. And Sadayya got the Inn fixed. And yet, I was mad with Sadayya. Mad at how easy it had been for the Lady Woodgrove to buy her off.

I realized I wanted Sadayya to fight to keep me in the Inn harder. What sense did wanting that make, when I was so eagerly packing my things to leave?

"I've lost Tia. Now it appears I'm losing you," Sadayya said softly. "The Inn will be the only thing I have left of my family."

I sealed the case and turned to face her.

She'd been crying. That almost made me reach around to start unpacking.

"I need to show you something," she said. "I know you want to go. I know I've... made this deal with Lady

Woodgrove. But I want you to watch something first."

She was up to something. I had to stay frosty cool, I thought, with a faint miasma of suspicion settling over me. Sadayya was trying to talk me into staying.

I rolled my eyes. "What now?" I said in an exasperated tone.

Sadayya pointed at one of my walls. It lit up.

Video of Lady Woodgrove walking at the foot of the gantries and cradles of a space port, one that dwarfed the tiny one on Sargasso, filled my room. Spires and flanges of giant sparships filled the horizon behind her.

"We're here to see famous interstellar traveler and guide: the Lady Amanda Woodgrove," an excited voice said. "Who is outfitting a new ship for a return to the battlefields of the *SparkFlint*. What new vistas and stories will we be able to experience about that mad old ship this time? Who knows, but we'll have the inside scoop!"

The video jumped, and we saw Lady Woodgrove standing in front of a large, round airlock studded with monitors.

"I categorically *deny* that we're looking for the *SparkFlint's* treasures," she said with a giant smile that suggested the complete opposite. "Only someone from the ship's crew would have any idea how to find such a thing."

More details followed. That Woodgrove had purchased a controlling share of an entire sparship called the *Dorado*, also known by the nickname *Carpe Per Diem* among a number of other sparship crew who consented to be interviewed. They appeared as ghostly abstract shapes on the screen, unwilling to give their identity up.

Word was already out among gossip networks that Lady Woodgrove been scouring the world for experiences interstellar crew that would be willing to leave right away.

"She's shuffled her crew, moving away from the adventurers of her previous expeditions in favor of a number of veterans from the Kai Hanimar conflicts. These are the sort of men who will be able to handle exploring old *SparkFlint* battlegrounds, where there are still active traps left around for unsuspecting treasure-hunters to stumble across."

Sadayya snapped her fingers and the wall faded back into being a wall again.

"Is it true?" She rested her head against the doorframe, a tired sharpness in her voice. "Any of it? What do I do, Jane? Battlefields? They're talking about battlefields!"

"Lady Woodgrove was never hurt on her other expeditions," I said. "She knows what she's doing. She has a team. And we have the doctor. And I have the map."

When I said that, she jerked up, looking at me with a sad puppy dog look. "The map." She pursed her lips.

She reached for my arm, and then stopped. As if she might get infected.

"I'm still disappointed with you. Maybe if I hadn't been so... distracted." She took a deep breath. "It's hard right now. Very tough."

"I just wanted to be able to manage the house systems," I told her. And see the public data layers out in the open, like everyone else.

"It's too late now, I guess," she said.

"It is," said Dr. Armstrong, moving in from the top of the stairs. "Second thoughts were for when you had that conversation with Lady Woodgrove. You had your moment to stop this, Sadayya. It has passed."

Sadayya faced him. "But it's not a secret voyage anymore, is it? It's not safe anymore."

Dr. Armstrong's mouth was a compressed line of fury. "Woodgrove is botching the mission's launch, yes. But no one else has the sheer resources to throw at making this a success. What you need to remember is this: if Jane stays here, she will be in far more danger than if she comes with us."

The riggers would come for me here. And then Sadayya would be in danger.

Staying wasn't an option.

I dragged the case off the bed. It was time to deliver the heavy stuff. "Mom..."

Sadayya stopped and turned to look at me. I didn't use that word often.

"I don't want to die, trapped here in the Inn. Or having never seen anything other than Sargasso's streets. It's dangerous. But so is sitting here, wondering if riggers will be back to try and destroy my mind when they come to pry this map out of it. And if this works out... if it works, we'll all be rich. As rich as Lady Woodgrove. And then they won't ever be able to harm us ever again."

She stood still, just staring at me. I walked up and kissed her on the cheek.

"Jane..."

"I love you," I said. "See you soon."

I grabbed Dr. Armstrong's arm. He was still frowning as I piloted him down the corridor as quickly as I could, without looking like I was running.

"Quick," I whispered at him. "Before any of us changes our mind."

We burst out into the cold air of the street, still speed-walking.

A bright orange taxi waited for us on the street. The large turbofan jets on stubby wings overhead were aimed down at the ground.

I flung my case in and followed it. Dr. Armstrong pulled the door down after the two of us.

"Canaveral," he ordered the taxi. "As fast as possible. I'll pay for fuel overages."

Data flickered to life across the front window-screen as the taxi powered on. A waterfall of numbers, maps, trajectories. Estimated times of arrival. The engines kicked dust through the street in front of the Inn and the hanging sign outside the Inn flapped about as the taxi rose into the air.

I looked down as we rose above the old Inn. Sadayya walked out of the front lobby and looked up at us. I waved, tentatively, and she just wrapped her arms around herself.

Dr. Armstrong rubbed his forehead. "I'm having a moment of doubt," he said.

"Doubt?" I asked.

"I'm not sure if I yanked you out of there so quickly because I truly believe I'm saving your life," he sighed. "Or if it's because I'm completely blinded by the idea of finding the *Sparkflint's* fortune."

I leaned forward and put a hand on his shoulder to reassure him. "Maybe it's both," I said.

"Maybe," he said with a frown.

Maybe.

I leaned against the window as twenty-four hours of delayed sleep crept toward me like a silvered fog that draped itself around the edges of my vision.

"What treasures do you think are really out there?" I asked. I felt like a kid again: sleep licking at the corners of my brain, settling over me like a favorite blanket. Someone telling me a story about wondrous, distant things, and adventures.

"We know the *Sparkflint* took precious metals. Jewels. Art. Programmable matter. Quantum entangled bits."

"Quantum bits?" Tiny little atoms, I thought. They were the same little atom, but existing in two places at the same time. Separated, you could take them as far apart as you wanted. Then use them for communication. Or other things. Once you flicked one, the other would imitate that action. And once you did that, they were un-entangled, or something like that. You could only use each one once, but it let you instantly send a message anywhere.

"Lady Woodgrove lost a fortune in a cargo of bits, stolen by the *Sparkflint*. The entangled side just sits in a bank vault of hers, useless without the other side. It's why she takes hunting the *Sparkflint* so seriously. A handful of bits would leave you richer than anyone in Sargasso," Dr. Armstrong said. "And there's more than a handful hidden away in the *Sparkflint's* trove."

Far below, I saw my city from above for the first time. Sargasso was all glittering steel; a flattened mirrored orb with long counterweights, power plants, and foundries swinging underneath.

It looked like a giant silvered jellyfish hanging in the air over the dull gray of the Atlantic Ocean.

And I was running away from the embrace of those long steel arms.

Chapter Twelve

Canaveral City sprawled like silver and green moss across the edge of Florida. Skyscrapers, tracks, walkways, and roads spilled around the ancient swamps and parks, then slipped off into the ocean. It even continued on underneath the ocean in some of the more exclusive neighborhoods, the underwater city lights shimmered under aquamarine waters.

"Have you been to Canaveral before?" I asked.

Armstrong nodded. "They don't call it the capital of the world for nothing," he mused.

Canaveral was one of the first places where people on Earth started striving to reach the depths of space. And it was right here where the depths of space reached back out when other worlds and other civilizations from the stars found Earth.

Most sparships landed here. Commerce between the rest of the Solar System, and further, mostly passed through here.

Canaveral was an epicenter of power.

I could feel it as I passed over the two-mile-high needle-tops of skyscrapers, saw it in the dense, crammed streets twined far below, and felt it in the explosion of people moving around below.

"Ah, we're almost there," Dr. Armstrong said.

The taxi weaved through several more buildings, and then rose up into the air past floating billboards that dripped with neon lights and active advertising plastered across their sides.

We landed on a taxi-pad a hundred stories up at the top of a square skyscraper near the edge of the famous Canaveral Docks.

Here Canaveral tapered away to swamp and greenfields. And there, in the old world, park-like grounds, rose the massive gantries and support structures that held massive sparships in their steely grips.

It looked like a harbor cluttered with masts, the water a grassy green. The hulls didn't gleam like the solarcell painted buildings around us. Sparship skin sucked away all the light into its matte black super-dense outer layers. As a result, they were like dark, brooding masses dominating the air over the greens of the docks.

Hundreds of ships hung lengthwise, others pointed straight up, all in gantries and all blocking out the sun underneath.

When they were sitting still.

One of the giant ships, easily the size of the very skyscraper we had landed on, shivered and shook free of its restraints, then rose up into the sky.

As it did so, long spars unfolded from flat against the hull.

Blocking out the sun for a moment, the spiked hull of the sparship coasted over the city. It paused, then sprinted for the clouds. It moved far too fast for its massiveness.

"Come on, Jane," Dr. Armstrong said firmly, opening the door to my side of the taxi. I gasped in welcome at the strong waves of heat that rolled over me. "Let's get moving."

I pulled my travel case free and hopped down. Dr. Armstrong released the taxi and it took off, circled around the building once, and merging into a stream of other flying taxis.

Shading my eyes I looked around. "I thought we were going to Lady Woodgrove's ship?"

"Air traffic isn't allowed to cross over the Docks. We're smuggling you aboard another way, so that we don't let anyone know we have you," Dr. Armstrong waved a hand toward a set of ornate, wooden doors with stained glass portholes. "With the help of Jonny Argyros."

"Jonny Argyros?"

Dr. Armstrong picked up his own suitcase and pointed ahead of him at the doors. I noticed the rusted, ancient metal ship's anchors bolted on the outsides under the window portholes. "He's one of Woodgrove's most trusted agents here. Argyros helped us a great deal on our last mission, looking for the *Sparkflint*, and he helped get a ship and crew at the last minute. He'll be an important part of the mission crew."

"He's a rigger?" I asked, stopping in front of the great doors.

The words SPYGLASS were decoratively burned into the doors by some sort of laser.

"Maybe. Once, long ago. Long ago." Dr. Armstrong's face twisted, as if recalling something uncomfortable. "He won't be a rigger, he'll be more of a quartermaster and advisor for this trip. He doesn't run ships anymore. These days, Argyros owns a destination club that caters to ship crews in the upper levels of this building. Very exclusive, limited sort of thing. "

"The Spyglass is very limited indeed," said someone in the shadows of the column to the right of the door.

His eyes glinted silver as he shifted, and then stepped out.

I flinched. While the left side of this man's face was handsome, in a grizzled and strong-jawed sort of way, the right side faded into a mirror image of the left. But it was made of the same matte black material as a sparship's hull instead of skin.

There were scars on his hands, and under his jaw. I could even see pulsing tubes of greenish fluid in the cords of his neck.

"Argyros," Dr. Armstrong greeted him with a raised hand.

Argyros smiled, but only with half his face. He gave a slight bow, throwing back the edges of his long, black leather coat as he did so. "I'm sorry. I didn't mean to startle you, I've been waiting for you to show," he said in a smooth voice. He looked over at me. "The Spyglass is the most exclusive club for discerning ship's crews in Canaveral. Dr. Armstrong is quite correct."

He handed me a business card. Not a physical one, but a virtual one that fluttered its way from his hands over to mine like a butterfly.

The card unfolded itself and began to list Argyros's

74

credentials.

He was the CEO of Spyglass. A member of the Canaveral City Council. A noted historian of the Kai Hanimar Conflicts.

There was more to the list, but before I could continue reading Argyros waved for my attention. "My security systems tell me flying paparozoids are trying to move in for a closer look at who just arrived," he announced. "Let's get you inside quickly."

I glanced up at the sky, and saw two shiny robotic discs hanging in the air between the landing pad jutting out of our skyscraper and the nearest building.

The air around us lit up with laser light and sparkles. An anti-photography shield.

"Come on, come," Argyros said, shooing us inside. "They'll try to jet in closer to beat the shield."

Two skeletal, metal humanoid robots stepped forward and matched Johnny Argyros's stride as he led us into the club. They stood on either side of Argyros, like bodyguards.

The Spyglass bulged out of the skyscraper underneath the landing pad. As if the building were a seagull's neck after the bird had snapped up a large, stiff cracker that had lodged in its gullet.

The great, distressed wooden doors swung open, and a blast of music struck us all square in the face. All around the edges of the club, large windows looked out over Canaveral's glittering skyline and the streets far below. Old, brass telescopes were mounted on a chrome rail that ran along the edge of the windows, letting anyone zoom in on the city.

"Am I even allowed to be in here?" I asked Dr. Armstrong, as I stared at a mostly nude woman with leopard-print skin and gold dust scattered on her cheeks.

The middle of the club was sunken, a shallow pit. Riggers jumped and danced and whirled in the spaces between mirrored columns, or lined up at the bar to smoke out of hookas. A haze of sweet-smelling smoke rose above the pit.

Half-naked Rigger men flickered as luminescent tattoos tapped out messages in code. Others favored dark cloaks. I saw silvered and dark black eyecaps everywhere.

I felt like they were all examining me. Studying me. I wondered if someone in that crowd might recognize me. Someone who might want to yank the secrets I was infected with out, and then kill me.

Dr. Armstrong startled me as he put a fatherly hand on my shoulder and kept me moving along. "Let's not tell your mother about this," he shouted over the music.

Argyros led us around the pit and through another set of doors leading into his private offices. These rooms where at the front of the Spyglass, and the large floor to ceiling windows looked out on the Canaveral Docks.

The loud music died, blocked by the doors as they closed and sealed behind us with a hiss.

"I have a…" Argyros started.

"…question to ask," the nearest robot said, turning the steel, eye-less face at me as it spoke in Argyros's voice and continued the second half of the sentence.

"I'm sorry?" The change in where the voice came from confused me. I wasn't sure where to look. Or why Argyros was doing this.

"Do either of you know a ship's crewperson by the name of the Black Dog?" asked the second robot.

My mouth dried. I thought back to Villem and his warnings. *Watch out for the three of them that walk like they're one…*

"Is something wrong?" Both the robots and Argyros had stopped with me, and all were looking at me with concern. I had taken a big step back, and I must have looked worried.

How did I ask this without telling Argyros about Villem, or insulting someone important to Lady Woodgrove?

"Your mind," I said. "It's in those robots as well, right? You're all three Johnny Argyros." I looked from the blank robotic face to Argyros's half-mangled, half matte-black visage. And half his mouth quirked in a smile.

"I'm sorry, I didn't explain earlier. It must seem alarming to some. It's actually not uncommon for some of the Kai Hanimar veterans," Argyros explained. "When the attack that seared off half my head came, my consciousness was spread throughout several machines I was managing in battle. My body was pretty mangled, but I was still what you might call 'operational.' Even without most of my old organic brain."

Not uncommon?

That relieved me. Would Lady Woodgrove hire a criminal rigger? No, she'd be doing background checks. She'd worked with Argyros before. Villem had probably been scared of some other space-ruined rigger with his brain spread out across a pair of machines.

"I'm sorry, I didn't know," I mumbled, realizing I'd started to panic about nothing. "And as for Black Dog, she attacked me back in the Inn. She was trying to get to Villem. Why do you ask?"

"She came nosing around the Spyglass, asking a lot of strange questions," Argyros said. The two metal versions of himself tapped their temples. "Got me wondering."

"When was this?" Dr. Armstrong asked.

Argyros inhaled. "I kicked her out of the Spyglass last night."

I glanced behind us at the doors separating us from the chaos of the nightclub and the Riggers inside. All those mechanical eyes, I thought.

"How many friends does Black Dog have out there, in your club?" I asked.

When I turned back, I found Argyros staring right at me with a laser-like intensity that almost made me take a step back.

"I won't lie to you, Jane," he said. "Black Dog's got people out there. People that'll know you've already stepped into the Spyglass and will be setting up plans to kidnap you. There will be people outside the building... watching. Waiting."

He let me digest that for a moment. I made a face.

Argyros smiled widely. "This whole expedition's been leaking info about our plans. It's too dangerous to sit still and wait any longer for more crew, or better provisions. I think we're best off if we get ourselves aboard that ship right now and get the hell out of Canavaral, don't you Dr. Armstrong?"

Dr. Armstrong nodded. Uncertainly at first. Then firmly. "I agree."

"There's a freight elevator that takes us to the store room. From there we'll smuggle aboard in a container destined for the ship," Argyros folded his arms.

"And Black Dog's friends?" I asked. "The ones that might be waiting outside for us?"

Johnny Argyros leaned forward with a wickedly wolfish smile. "Oh, Miss Hawkins, I have no doubt they *will* be waiting. And that is a contingency I have prepared for."

Chapter Thirteen

Deep in the plasticated concrete bowels of the skyscraper Johnny Argyros escorted us to an armored truck. Two riggers, heavily suited up in matte-black, mechanically powered external armor, followed the truck on bulky bikes.

"That's Benji, and Harrison. They're well-rated mercenaries that have traveled with the Lady Woodgrove," Dr. Armstrong explained to me.

As we glided through the streets of Canaveral I watched Argyros pull down skeins of data from the air. It was all information from outside the truck. There were cameras photographing every face outside, matching them against known rigger crews.

The two metal robots on either side of Argyros stared at the incoming data. Looking for possible threats.

But Argyros's human self leaned forward. Through the bulletproof glass he pointed toward the Canaveral Docks. "See that ship? That's the *Cheerful Cthonic Surprise.*"

His finger glowed with extra data that appeared just for my eyes. It all highlighted one of the mile-long, needle-like sparships at rest between a crab-like gantry.

Cheerful Cthonic Surprise glowed, and a sheet of information unrolled. The ship's resume crystallized for me. I could see the routes it had traveled, and that it was looking for crew for a new two hundred light year long jaunt that it was getting refurbished for.

"Over there is the *Outer Limits*, she's taking passengers for Alpha Centauri next week," the robot on the left said in Argyros's voice. "And that, the diamond-shaped one there, that's the *Not So Trivial After All.*"

I tried to reach up into the air and find more information about it, but the air rippled around that ship.

Argyros smiled as I tried to find any markers, or information about the *Not So Trivial After All.*

"A ship of war, Jane," said a blank black faceshield to his right. "You won't find anything about that one. Been decommissioned ever since the *Sparkflint* advanced on Earth."

I should have been thrilled. These were names right out of the most exciting stories I'd stayed up late for back in the Inn. But, somehow the blurred, hulking presence at the edge of the Docks didn't feel legendary, just slightly sinister.

Argyros's two robotic selves sat up straighter.

"What is it?" Dr. Armstrong asked.

"An alarm. Someone associated with Black Dog. Probably nothing," Argyros muttered.

I looked out through the thick windows, wondering which anonymous face out in the crowd was the one trying to kill us.

"Ah. I see them," Dr. Armstrong said. "They're moving at us."

I saw someone walking swiftly away, hands pushed deep inside a long coat's pockets.

It was Canaveral. Warm and muggy. Not the bitter cold of Sargasso. No one needed a coat here.

"Benji, Harrison, check it out," Dr. Armstrong ordered.

I watched the two of them get off their bikes through the heavy windows in the rear door. Their helmets swiveled to find their target.

The man in the coat spun around and pulled out massive gun.

A brief flash. A tiny rocket sprung forward, and the street behind the truck exploded before I could even react. I had a scream bubbling up in me, but it was cut short with a sort of gurgle of surprise when Harrison hit the back of the truck, thrown clear by the explosion. His armor dented the door.

I crouched in place on the bench, not sure whether putting my hands up in the air would even do anything to help protect me.

"Armor's holding," Harrison reported, his voice winded

and suddenly in my ear as he used a public channel to talk to everyone.

"I'm going after the bastard," Benji snapped. He came walking out of a cloud of debris, shaking pieces of road off his armor. "Get to the ship, we'll catch up."

"Security drones and Canaveral police are inbound," the driver reported.

"Then let's not tarry," Argyros said.

"We can't leave them," I said, finding my voice.

And then I had a second, more selfish, thought. We would be vulnerable without our bodyguards. But Argyros was already thinking about that. He kicked open the rear door and his two metallic selves jumped out and shut the doors behind them.

The truck weaved through stalled out vehicles, and then once in the clear, accelerated for the docks with the two robots running along behind it.

I looked over at Dr. Armstrong, who looked a little pale.

Out of the back of the truck, through the cracked bulletproof glass, Benji and Harrison dwindled away as they fanned out to start the search for the attacker.

Argyros leaned forward and looked at me. "Are you okay?"

"They're really after me, aren't they?" I looked down at my shaking hands. I could hear Dr. Armstrong talking to someone on the *Dorado* in a rattled-but-forcing-calm-anyway sort of voice.

"They were trying to peel off our protection," Argyros said. "Looking for an opening."

"Thank you," I said. Argyros had a distant, far off look of pained concentration. He was coordinating half of himself running along behind the truck and talking to me at the same time.

A satisfied grin quirked his lips. "No need to thank me," he said. "And here's dock-side security."

Three blue drones kicked up street dust as they dropped out of the sky and paced the truck. The canyons of steel skyscrapers faded away.

We passed under the shadows of slumbering giant hulls of sparships, and I stared up awkwardly through the windows at the bellies of the great, star-faring ships in their berths until we lurched to a stop underneath the *Dorado*.

It was a castle to hide inside. Here I would be safe. And soon I'd be leaving the dangers and troubles the old dead rigger had forced onto me.

I'd be leaving them all behind faster than light itself could travel.

We rode up into the open bays of the *Dorado* via an open platform that dropped down to the ground by thick, snake-like cables.

A rigger waited for us. This one's eyes glinted all blue, and he wore a tight-fitting, red uniform with pockets on the arms and thighs. A neat series of square glyph tattoos over his left eyebrow unpacked in my vision.

His name was Captain Garrik.

A list of ships that he'd served aboard as captain began to pile up in my vision.

"Captain," said Johnny Argyros and tapped his head. He smiled. The two robots on either side of him swept their hands at me and said together; "the last of your cargo is on ship and safe."

"Thank you Mr. Argyros."

Deep inside the twilight of the ship's cargo bay, I felt a heaviness roll off my shoulders. The fear of the attack on the street had been added to the fear I had been carrying about the attack on the Inn. I hadn't realized how unsafe I'd felt. How tense I'd been.

But now my shoulders straightened and I stood up just a bit taller, no longer weighed down by something I hadn't realized I'd been carrying.

Underneath us the ship's bay doors rumbled shut, sealing the belly of the ship against the outside world. Massive lights flickered on overhead, burning away the gloom with white hot interior light. I expected gleaming white corridors and fresh paint. But the bay looked like the inside of an old warehouse. Chains hung from the rusted out ceiling on greasy block and tackle that had been used to move cargo cubes around the bay.

The walls were streaked with dirt and grease, and the metal lattice under our feet peeled paint. The cargo cubes were battered old plastic, and some of them had been covered in graffiti, both real and virtual.

The captain raised a hand and the Lady Woodgrove appeared as a hologram between us all. "I told you I couldn't come down there in person," she said with an irritated wave. "I have three more interviews. Oh, hello Armstrong, and Miss Hawkins. I take it you're all aboard now?"

I gaped. Hadn't she been paying attention to anything that had been going on?

Captain Garrik looked disgusted. His lip twitched. "I called this meeting because I'm not happy about the state of this expedition," he said grimly. "Particularly after this attack. I've cancelled the flight plan, I'm putting this mission on hold. At the least."

I stared at him. We had survived a rigger attack in the streets of Canaveral to end up grounded here? So close to launch?

Chapter Fourteen

L ady Woodgrove had been playing around with something offscreen. She stopped, her sharp face swiveling to stare at the captain. "What *exactly* is your concern?" she asked in an icy voice.

"Concerns," Captain Garrik said. "Plural."

"Are there any problems with the ship?"

"The *Dorado*'s in excellent shape. I've perused the last ultrasounds of her hull. She's fit. The internal systems are old, but capable. The spars have been replaced and can handle the journey. The service record is impeccable."

Lady Woodgrove folded her arms and looked down her nose. "If the ship is fine, then what's your problem?"

"Easy, Amanda," Dr. Armstrong muttered. "He's the captain, it's his job to raise concerns."

She ignored him. As did the captain, who was matching her fiery stare with a laconic calm. "I signed a non-disclosure agreement that said if I even hinted at what kind of equipment we were loading, and where we might be going, I'd end up in some heinous legal trouble. And I wasn't told specifically where we were going due to confidentiality concerns."

"Yes—" Lady Woodgrove started to interrupt.

The captain continued, ignoring her. "And *yet*, almost everyone who follows your adventures seems to have been let in on the secret that you're not just on another, normal travel jaunt. It's common knowledge you are going after the *Sparkflint*'s treasure. Does it even make sense I'm still under an NDA now?"

"No," said Dr. Armstrong, looking at Lady Woodgrove's holographic image. "It doesn't, does it?"

Woodgrove threw up her hands. "Okay. We'll cancel your NDA."

She didn't sound very sorry to me. More annoyed and

petulant. But then, when you were as rich as the Lady Woodgrove, people had to put up with whatever mood you were in. You didn't have to hide it and worry about what people thought.

"This isn't some travel show about exotic destinations," Captain Garrik said. "We're going after something dangerous. Something that wouldn't have surrendered it's treasures lightly. In situations like that, we need to know that crew minds are all working together as one. And I hardly know any of our crew."

"You're complaining about crew *now*?" Lady Woodgrove asked. "We're ready to go."

Captain Garrik gritted his teeth. "This is the first time I've been able to speak to you, Lady, about my concerns. You've been too busy. This is a sparship. These riggers will all be melding to the ship's network to manage spars up and down the hull. I should have been involved with picking them. It's a captain's right."

Dr. Armstrong looked over at Lady Woodgrove. "I thought these were all handpicked men?"

"They were," she said. "By Argyros."

Argyros had been observing the argument, but doing his best to remain standing on the edge of the group with a poised, carefully neutral expression on his face.

"I'm only familiar with a handful of them," Captain Garrik said. "And have worked with even fewer."

"Argyros knows crew better than almost anyone else," Lady Woodgrove said, waving toward the man and the two human-shaped robots flanking him. "I've worked with him before. *You're* the new one to the team."

Argyros's two robots shifted from foot to foot uncomfortably, and Argyros looked pained.

"No offense, John. But..." Captain Garrik took a deep breath. "You can all captain your own damn ship. We all have to work as one, become a single mind through the neural taps controlling the ship. That's tricky business. It's matter of trust, and control. I clearly don't have either here. I can't be an effective captain. So I'll have to give you my resignation."

Putting up with Lady Woodgrove's arrogance was one thing. Letting her scuttle the entire mission right in front of me was another. I stepped forward, not even sure how I was going to fix this. But I had to try.

"Captain, please," I grabbed his arm. "The longer we sit here, the longer those riggers that tried to kill me will have to keep trying to get at the ship."

He wavered.

"Do you have family of your own?" I asked him.

He didn't answer, just looked away from me slightly.

Dr. Armstrong must have felt a space open. He smiled. "The crew aboard this ship, I've looked over their resumes. They're quite capable. I understand that you will be needing to trust them in split micro-seconds while we're traveling faster than the speed of light itself. The captain is the nerve center of the ship. I know we're asking a lot. But we need your help."

"I want a high order security background check of all the men," Captain Garrik said. "Get that to me, and I'll take this ship off the ground. In particular I want a close check of our Information Systems Executive."

"Mr. Arrow?" Lady Woodgrove asked. "Why is that?"

"Take a look at the back of his neck some time," Argyros spoke up, apparently agreeing with the Captain. "The transdermal patches he's using aren't authorized by the Captain, and he's not getting them from the ship's infirmary. I take the blame, he came with high recommendations, but I see the captain's concerns."

Captain Garrick looked surprised that Argyros was agreeing with him. "Yes. Check him out. Do the highest level background checks. I'll drill the crew once more. If we pass the synchronization tests and my ISE comes back clean, then we're a go."

"I'll do the checks," Lady Woodgrove said frostily.

Garrick left us standing together by shipping cubes stored in the bay.

"I think I chose our captain too hastily," Lady Woodgrove muttered.

"It's a captain's right to pick his crew," Dr. Armstrong said. "Matter of principle. You just don't like it because he's right. But I think, between Argyros and Garrick, we have a good team helping us."

Woodgrove sneered and faded away.

We stood in the bay hatch for a moment, listening to the tick-tick-tick of dripping water somewhere in the distance. The crew dragged cargo cubes into place and latched them down into place with magnetic locks.

"I better go calm her down a bit," Dr. Armstrong muttered. "Argyros, can you show Jane to her room?"

"Not a problem," Argyros said. One of his robots watched as Dr. Armstrong left, while Argyros's human self regarded me with friendly interest.

When Armstrong got out of range, Argyros stepped forward. "Are they sleeping together?"

I burst out laughing. It was relief that it looked likely we would launch, and it was also at Argyros's just coming right out and asking. My laugh echoed over the tops of stacked, locked together cubes and around the several hundred feet of bay storage. "I have no idea," I said to Argyros with a grin.

"Well," he said with a shy shrug. "I just wondered."

"If I find out," I said conspiratorially, "I'll let you know."

"Okay," he said. His two robots moved into place behind us as he led me out of the bay. There were central corridors up and down the ship. They were clean, almost sparkling compared to the storage bay, but still bore the marks of age and use. Pipes ran along the ceilings in between bulkheads. Easy-to-remove grating clanged under our feet as we moved along.

"I want to learn what riggers do," I told Argyros. "I'll be on the ship. Can I watch? Can you teach me to join that melding of minds?"

Being part of a rigger crew was supposed to be a thrilling melding of the minds. I could hardly sit on a ship with all the modifications forced onto me and not take advantage of them.

Argryos shook his head. "Armstrong and Woodgrove would kill me."

I gritted my teeth.

And Argyros continued. "Besides, that life is long behind me. They won't let someone damaged like I was get into the shared neural space of a running ship."

"Oh," I said. I'd forgotten that. "Why not?"

"My mind is spread out between these machines, in addition to my body. It's natural for me. People fear I would install parts of myself into the ship's utilities. Become something larger and inhuman."

"Like the *Sparkflint*," I said.

"Yes. So you really have to talk to one of the crew," Argyros said conversationally.

I followed him through the flickering lights and metal corridors, disappointed.

Argyros kept talking, though. He took me by the shoulder and lowered his voice. "The crew have some training and certification programs they would probably be able to be talked out of."

"Oh!" I said, now hopeful, and realizing what he was doing.

He smiled at me. "I'll tell the captain you're working with me, and learning your implants. You'll find my office near the kitchen. Here's your room."

I had to push on a old, manual latch to swing the thick door open to my cramped little cove. I put my bags under the bunk bed.

"Will I have to help out in the kitchen? Why are you near the kitchen?" I asked. Wouldn't it just suck to get all the way away from the Inn and Sargasso, off to explore the universe, just to have to clean up after breakfast again?

Argyros leaned against the entrance to my room with one hand. "I'm the quartermaster, Jane. It's a step down from what I was doing in Canaveral, but it's the best way for me to get aboard a ship as I'm not a rigger anymore. I provision the ship. Make sure your favorite foods are aboard. Account for the other supplies. It's mostly automated, though, I'm not going to put you to hard work washing dishes." He glanced around the room. "And as the quartermaster, I should say, let me know if you need anything, Jane."

"Thank you." I sat on the small bed and looked up at him. It was a good thing Lady Woodgrove had him as an old friend. "And thank you for telling me about the training programs."

He tapped the side of the doorframe. "Keep that our secret," he smiled, and the three pieces of him clanked off down the corridor.

It was a shame they couldn't fire Garrik and put Johnny Argyros in as captain. Argyros seemed the kind to lead us all right to the hidden treasures with confidence.

But now, with his brain spread out across himself and those two robots, no one wanted him plugging into the ship.

Our loss.

A distant hum threaded through the mass of the ship. I looked up at the flaking paint on the pipes above my bunk. They shivered and vibrated. Something powerful had turned on deep in the ship's spine.

I stood up, excited, and put my hand against the wall.

It felt like a thousand deep voices, droning in chant near my fingertips. Or a hundred, muted and distant thunderstorms contained tight within a metallic heart.

Footsteps clanked down outside my room. I darted outside and found a rigger bolting past. I ran after him.

Richard Johnson, read a tag over his head. Virtual threads hung from his head, tickling the walls like a ghostly Medusa's head. Informational dreadlocks, I thought, thinking of the tightly wound locks of my own slapping my neck as I ran after him.

I ran down the core of the ship, through yet another small bay, and the kitchens. I waved at Argyros, who waved back.

Sweaty and out of breath, the rigger found his spot. An alcove built into the side of the hull. A large chair nestled deep into the carved out piece of hull. Around it was a halo of mechanical clutter and junk: pipes, cables that dripped coolant from their tips, old screens flickering data in old formats in case of failure.

"Why'd you follow me?" he asked as he sat down. The chair's arms swiveled, turned into padded restraints, and hugged him tight.

He pulled a coolant cable down and plugged it right into the back of his neck with a puff of cold mist. Another cable glittered with fiber-optic light: a direct connection to the raw computing power of the entire ship.

Richard glowed in the virtual world, symbols dropping out from his skin to indicate that his now upgraded neural capacity had increased by several factors.

He snapped his head in my direction. "Youbettergetstrappedin," he said.

"What?" I could barely follow the sounds.

"Takeoff."

All the lights through the *Dorado* flipped off, and then turned back on in a dim and somewhat ominous red. "All hands, all crew, all passengers," Garrik's gritty voice pounded through the corridors and bulkheads. His words appeared in the air as well, glowing and bright announcements. "Prepare for departure."

"Do I really need to strap in?" I asked. The *Dorado* wasn't some early sparship, struggling to manage the invisible currents. It was a modern ship.

Then I looked up at the peeling paint on a nearby bulkhead.

Delete that. It was a *mostly*-modern ship.

I looked around, wondering where there was another spot to get strapped in. Richard snapped his fingers and pointed. A bench slid out from under the screens in front of him. Straps jiggled from the hard wall.

There'd been a loud buzzing in the back of my head. I suddenly realized it was Dr. Armstrong trying to get in touch with me. This virtual neural stuff was still new to me. "Dr. Armstrong?"

His ghostly face appeared, superimposed over my

surroundings. "Jane, you're not in your room. Where are you? Are you okay?"

"I'm okay," I said. "I'm with one of the sparmen, I wanted to watch us take off."

"Make sure you're strapped in!"

"Oh come on," I protested. "It can't be that bad. If any real acceleration leaked through we'd all be crushed by it. We're going to be going faster than light!" When the ship dipped its spars out, they'd catch and sling it up to unimaginable speeds.

In the old days, anyone inside would have been destroyed. Only robots and cyborgs could handle interstellar travel.

But then the Kai Hanimar had sold humanity technology that would let people ride inside ships.

"Port Authority won't let us accelerate like that until we're well clear of the Earth's atmosphere," Dr. Armstrong lectured. "We'll be bumping around in the air first, and so you'll need strapped in. Just in case. Or you can stand around and take your chances. I guess I can patch you up afterwards if we pass through any turbulence."

Suitably chastened, I sat down on the tiny jump seat Richard had pointed me at.

We sat knee to knee.

Up close, I could smell ozone and peaches. His skin was so pale it was almost sallow. Corpse-like. Someone who rarely stood under the light of a real sun.

His eyes had faded entirely to black, with tiny bits of green numerals reflected in them from the old screens around us. He smiled, and his filed metal teeth clicked. The cables draped around his shaved head pulsed with coolant veins.

"*Gonnaneedaspedafowmin*," Richard grunted, wriggling even further into his comfortable seat.

"What?"

He didn't reply. His fingers were twitching, a blur.

I kept staring at them, trying to follow along. They were throwing pieces of windows around, tapping things faster than I could see.

Straining, I thought if I could just focus hard enough I might be able to see what he was doing.

I shivered violently.

The last time that had happened I'd been speeding myself up without realizing it, overheating biological processors grown and embedded in my cortex by Villem.

I touched the top of my head, and felt the feverish heat.

"Damn girl, use the cooling helmet before you fry yourself," Richard said. He spoke quickly, but I could follow it now.

"Where is it?"

"Rightbehindyou," he said. He was moving away from me, brain speeding even further up.

I fumbled around and found it. It hadn't looked like a helmet because it was more like a translucent skin hanging from the end of a cooling tube among the other straps behind me.

On my head it startled me by wriggling around. Tiny, gecko-like feelers sunk through my locks and found the scalp underneath. Then the feelers spread, moving around the hair to fill in until I had what now probably looked like a blue helmet.

It massaged my head and neck, coolant running down and around tiny capillaries and pulling the heat from my skull, neck, and shoulders.

"Here we go," Richard said. He pointed at the hull-side of the niche. The solid matter faded to transparency as the ship rearranged the nature of the hull, making it a screen that displayed the dense conglomeration of Canaveral City.

The *Dorado* rose above the docks, its shadow covering other ships below as it moved along overhead.

I could see that Richard had moved the spar he controlled out. There were overlays hanging between us. A wind tore through everything around us, though it disturbed nothing.

"You see the winds?" Richard asked. Thousands of times a second the spar trimmed itself, hundreds of flaps twisting and turning to keep just the right amount dipped into the wind.

I nodded as the *Dorado* spiraled up into the clouds, leaving Canaveral far below. I rattled about in the straps as the ship hit some turbulence passing through a large thunderstorm. Clouds darkened the world outside, and lightning danced along the spars sticking out randomly from the hull.

"Only riggers see the winds," Richard said distractedly. He was focused on the spar. "Takes a lot of computation to be able to represent that, and you have to be fast."

The winds ripped through the entire universe, and had been invisible to human science. But not, apparently, to alien minds that first found out, then traded knowledge about it, through the galaxy.

The wind changed, an eddy rippling through it all. Richard ducked the spar in slightly, the *Dorado* shivered, and then surged as a command flitted through all sparmen. I could sense it. I had the software buried somewhere in the back of my neck. The captain ordered more speed, and the ship climbed out through the tallest of the clouds.

The cities below were metal grids and, in the distance, patterns of lights.

The atmosphere faded from blue to purple. Blackness seeped into everything. The Earth turned into a sphere.

"We are clear, permission granted for full spar deployment," Captain Garrik reported to the entire ship. His words sounded slow and syrupy. If he was as sped up as I was right now, it was just theatrics for the non-riggers aboard.

"And…"

I watched Richard dip the spar all the way into the ethereal wind. A bubble of energy rippled to surround the ship, and the world shifted around us. Everything shifted from around us to move up front, compacted into torus of light.

"Go!"

The *Dorado* was ripping through the universe faster than the speed of light, riding a wave of invisible current out to a destination buried in my new, refactored DNA.

Chapter Fifteen

The *Dorado* slowly rose out of the solar system, streamers of invisible energy spinning off from its spars as they dipped further and further into the universe's ghostly winds. I left the very world I'd been born on further and further behind with every split second.

This was the first day of an entirely new life. I had escaped the troubles Villem Osteonidus had dropped on me. And I now had everything he had gifted me as well.

I looked at Richard, twitching as he kept the spar balanced and primed, responding to the needs of the other spars, the structure of the ship, and the captain's orders.

This was where I belonged. Out here. Leaving Earth far behind me.

I wanted to do what he was doing. I leaned forward and said, "Richard, Argyros told me you have training software you could give me."

The all-black eyes flicked to regard me, as if seeing me for the first time. For a long moment Richard didn't respond as the words trickled down through his intense concentration. "That's for certifying riggers, girl."

"I know." I chose to ignore the diminutive 'girl.' For now.

He remained focused on the task at hand for another full minute while I stared directly at his pale, pink lips and waited. They finally curled slightly. "You think just because you got upgraded with some fancy neurals you're ready to ride a spar?"

"Yes."

He raised a hand, withdrawing the spar into the ship. All throughout the *Dorado* the mechanical thunks of most of the spars sliding smoothly into their berths shook the hull.

We coasted, now. But coasting in space wasn't like coasting on Earth, where you slowed down. Out in the vacuum there was little to slow the *Dorado*.

Captain Garrik appeared virtually outside the niche. "Jane, we're no longer at maximum spar. We'd like you in the cockpit as soon as possible."

It was time for the living map to make an appearance.

He faded away without even waiting for my reply. A glowing line appeared in the air with arrows jabbing in the direction of the cockpit.

I unbuckled and stood up, then turned back to Richard.

"You haven't answered me yet," I said, sliding the cooling helmet off with a sucking sound.

He folded his arms and propped his legs up on the jump seat. "You're going to overheat," he said. "You should step down, now, before you get addicted to remaining sped up. You still have the choice to rarely use it ahead of you."

The heat dizzied me. But he was still plugged in to the coolant tubes and would be speaking too fast to understand if I didn't stay like this.

At least until I got the answer I wanted.

We stared at each other until I had to grab the edge of the niche to steady myself.

"It was Argyros that told you I had certification simulators?" Richard finally asked.

"Yes."

Richard smiled. It was a predatory glint. "He seems to like you. Well, there it is. If you want to get into one of those simulators you'll have to do something for me."

I took a wobbly step back. "What is that?" I asked suspiciously.

"Get me some raw meat," he said.

Repulsed, I made a face. "Why the hell would I do that? What's wrong with normal stuff?"

"It isn't normal," Richard said. "Vat-grown. We're *used* to it. Yes. But I had a taste of the real thing on a planet where they grow cows. It's a delicacy for some of us crew."

"Where am I going to get a piece of *dead cow*?" I asked.

"Argyros," Richard said.

"Argyros?" Now I was doubly disgusted.

"He has a secret."

Heat rippling off my scalp, I leaned closer. "A secret?"

"A modified tiger, with a shard of his own mind. He feeds it real meat. You find Argyros's kitty, you'll find my meat. I get the meat, you get inside the simulation."

I let out a deep breath, and then started stepping myself down. I had to breathe deep and push my mind back into itself. I had to find the same stillness inside that it took to stand with the invisibility scarf on and not be seen.

Then, shivering, I stumbled my way toward the bridge.

Chapter Sixteen

ater and sludge trickled down from the walls,
heading for nooks and crannies in the ship below
me. However when I got there, the inside of the
cockpit gleamed like something from a fancy commercial. All
white and plush, holograms of stars hanging in the air, and
everywhere around the sight of dark space on sceens.

The cockpit itself was a transparent blister on the top of
the *Dorado* that looked over the entire ship.

It was a hell of a view.

"Oh good," Lady Woodgrove said, seeing me. "You got
here okay?"

She looked at me the way I imagined a dragon looked at a
gold chalice.

"Some people can get turned around when a ship gets
underway," she said in a cheerful tone. "Instead of down being
toward the belly, down is now toward the aft of the ship."

The inside of the *Dorado* had reoriented. I'd been
strapped in and focused on Richard and the spars, and my
perception of up and down had shifted about as we'd flung
ourselves into space. Now the ship was laid out like a
skyscraper because it was accelerating. There were just enough
spars dipped in to keep acceleration going, so it felt like there
was gravity in the ship. The floors I'd walked on earlier were
now walls with easy-to-remove grated panels.

"It wasn't that big of a deal," I said, truthfully. I'd been
expecting it.

Lady Woodgrove looked disappointed. "Oh."

I wiped sweat off my forehead, and worried that Dr.
Armstrong would notice the stains on my shirt. But he had the
same hungry look as Woodgrove.

Their minds were brimming with treasure.

"Coordinates?" Captain Garrik stepped forward. He was

attached to a series of coolant tubes that trailed from his spine, making him look like a steel porcupine. But unlike Richard, he spoke clearly and calmly to the normal passengers standing in his cockpit.

And yet, I realized, sniffing the digital air around him, he was coordinating a third of all the sparmen right now. A part of his mind orchestrated everything happening around us.

Captain.

I sucked in filtered air and stood up straight. Centered myself. The tattoos beneath my skin stirred. A blue haze trickled from inside me, then rushed out.

I blazed in the blue light, a cold virtual beacon for a moment, and then entered the navigation space Villem had infected me with.

"Do you have it, Mr. Garrik?" I asked, nervous that I might somehow be the only one that could still see it.

But that was happily not the case.

"Yes," he said. There was a distance in his voice now. The cool professionalism had been swept away like sand in a storm by the pinpricks of light I shared with the cockpit.

The *Dorado* shifted, spars sliding out to grip the universal winds and curve the sparship's path slowly into a new direction.

"With a single order, the journey begins," Captain Garrik whispered softly.

I waved the world of data away. The stars and symbols faded like ocean mist in the midday sun.

The way everyone in the cockpit looked, you would have thought I'd taken a child's favorite toy away. But I had other things to do than light up like a magic lantern for them. Besides, now that I'd given everyone here on the cockpit what they wanted, they didn't seem all that interested in me anymore. Garrik was focused on flying his ship. Doctor Armstrong and Lady Woodgrove muttered to each other, unable to hold back their excitement.

I was a part of this venture. But I wasn't a doctor, or the owner of Sargasso City. Already rich beyond imagining. How much of whatever treasures we found would be shared with me? Enough that I could figure out how to stay *out here*? Who knew? Who knew if we would even find anything. Maybe that was cynical of me, but it seemed that the doctor and the lady in some ways were struck stupid by the idea the riches ahead.

It was time to unpack my bags, find my scarf, and see if I could figure out how to find some raw meat.

***

I shadowed Argyros. He filed reports and checked manifests at his desk for two long, incredibly boring and taxing, hours. When he got up, looked around, and headed for the storage bays in the belly of the *Dorado* I almost broke and sighed with relief.

But that would have negated the effects of the scarf, sending out its constant visual lies to anyone with altered eyes.

I followed Argyros, playing the most excruciating game of red light, green light. When he walked, I followed him barefoot and carefully. When he stopped, I froze. When he looked back, I froze.

He didn't seem to suspect a thing. And remembering Villem's uncanny abilities and my own new ones, I stayed as far back away from Argyros as I dared.

In fact, I didn't go into the cargo bay with him. I waited outside until, half an hour later, his three selves clumped past me.

After he walked clear down the corridor, I opened cargo hold twelve's doors and stepped in.

Gloomy lights dappled thirty shipping cubes, the smart metal exteriors keeping the contents at their preferred temperature and humidity. The cubes advertised their contents to me with translucent pop ups and menus. A week ago I would have stopped to stare at the manifests but now I ignored them.

Deeper into the hold I wandered, until I stopped before a wall of cubes stacked five away from the wall.

I'd heard something behind them.

A rustle.

The pad of feet.

I kept still and triggered the scarf's software with a finger swipe. I held my breath and listened.

Click click click.

There was something hidden away in that island of cubes. And it wasn't a person. Now that I'd stopped and paid attention, I could feel the thud of each step in the hold's metal floor.

I clambered up the cubes, using small insets in the corners for machines to grab as my footholds. They were only stacked three high, and each cube was just about as tall as I was.

At the top I froze when I looked over.

A large orange tiger with green stripes paced in the twenty foot square enclosure. It sniffed the air angrily, sensing I was close. But apparently its eyes were keyed into public data, because it couldn't see me.

And I liked it that way.

Alarms sounded, whooping in the air. I jumped, despite myself, as Captain Garrik's voice snapped out an order: "All call medical alert! All qualified respondents to Mr. Arrow's office. Repeat, all medical to Mr. Arrow's office."

I looked back down and into the tiger's unblinking eyes. It sat on its bony haunches, looking straight up at me.

Busted.

I turned around to jump back down. Something struck the cube behind me.

Tick. Tick. Thud.

I didn't want to turn around. I'd made a mistake. I'd assumed the cubes penned the tiger in. That it couldn't jump this high.

But it had.

I, very slowly, turned around to face the tiger behind me. Yellowed eye to eye, the whiskers twitched only three feet away from my nose.

It huffed fishy breath, and every single ounce of me

realized that I was potential lunch. It hurt to breath, and my heart pounded so hard against my chest I could hear it.

"WHAT YOU DO HERE?" The words floated in the air between us as text.

I couldn't stop thinking about the fact that I was a gigantic walking steak, but managed to stammer, "Looking for meat."

"MEAT?" It sat down and licked its jaws. "PIECES OF MEAT?"

I nodded. "Argyros gives them to you, right? I was hoping to get some."

I didn't know what this tiger was. Some exotic pet, rammed full of neural upgrades to give it access to language? Or yet another shard of Argyros? One he couldn't have wandering around with him.

If it was a piece of Argyros, he would soon find out I'd stolen his weird delicacy.

"PIECES OF MEAT," the tiger agreed. "SHOW YOU. YOU GIVE ME."

It leapt down and padded through the maze of cubes outside of its pen, with me following. We stopped in front of a storage cube. The contents listed themselves for me: green beans, kale, and a lot of other things few people would miss.

"PIECES OF MEAT," the tiger said, nudging the cube with its head excitedly. The cube shifted and moved an inch from the enthusiastic head butt. "GIVE ME, TOO."

Ah, I realized as I figured it out how to open the cube. The tiger was in on the theft as well. As long as I shared my haul.

When I tossed the tiger his share, it ripped through the packaging to the raw slab of animal inside and began licking it like a meat popsicle. "PIECES OF MEAT," it said again into the air, and rumbled happily. "PLANS WITHIN PLANS."

"Good kitty," I said, and left before it got bored with its treat.

Chapter Seventeen

I found Richard in his niche sipping an energy drink and looking over complicated schematics in the air around him. He'd slowed himself down and unhooked from the coolant hoses.

He looked up, startled, when I shoved the two pounds of frozen meat through his diagrams at him. "What the hell?"

"I want to try the simulator now," I said.

"Where am I going to store two pounds of frozen meat?" he asked.

He hadn't really expected me to find and retrieve it. It had been something funny to send me off to try and do. Well…

"That's not my problem," I told him.

Richard reached out and petted the packaging, his mouth slightly open.

"Right," he said. "Right. You wait here."

He snapped his fingers and disappeared the schematics he'd been studying, cleaning the virtual air between us. He snatched the package away as he scrambled up to walk off down the corridor.

"When do I start the simulator?" I asked.

"After I hide this," he called over his shoulder.

Triumph!

***

Fifteen minutes later I sat in the jump seat again, coolant helmet digging into my dreadlocks as Richard booted up a set of sequences that cleared out the public data around us and replaced it with a facsimile of the real.

"So here's your spar." Richard handed a virtual slab of controls over to me. "Depth of spar deployment, angle of alignment, width of flaps…"

I pointed. "What's with the kittens?"

Rows and rows of tiny pink noses stared happily back at me with large, liquid eyes from above the controls.

"Those are spar condition indicators," Richard said.

"I swear if you chose kitty-cats because I'm the one doing this simulator I'm going to…"

"Those are my kittens," Richard said.

"*Your* kittens?" Momentarily stupefied I looked around the controls to make sure he wasn't joking around with me.

"Most people use human faces. Each face represents the health of various subsystems in the spar. Neurotypical humans are cognitively wired to understand facial expressions at a glance, rather than complex readouts. You can read a crowd just by glancing at it better than hundreds of dials and lights."

"Those aren't faces. They're cute digital kitties." Some of them had bows.

"I find the kittens easier to scan at a glance."

Each kitten was tagged. Structural stress points, temperature, potential power, contact with the universal wind ripping through us all.

"You know, after a certain point, it's kind of creepy," I muttered.

"Change it to anything you want," he said.

I swapped them out for points of light, green for normal and red for trouble. My board lit up green, along with a visual representation of a spar lying flat and inactive against the hull.

"I'm going to add wind, now," Richard said. "Ready?"

"Go."

My world filled with a tempest of silent wind. This was no simple representation of something from the real. It was a machine taking something hidden and almost unexplainable, and trying to cram down into my own human mind.

But I could feel it. A blistering force running through everything. A wind blasting through the universe in the vast space that existed between atoms and nuclei.

Richard let me sit there and experience it. He dropped the

Dorado away from around me, turning it transparent so that I
was sitting in nothingness with him across from me, the
emptiness of space compacted forward into a bright disk.

"That's the starbow up there," he said, a lecturing tone
creeping into his voice.

"Yeah, I know," I said. "The ship's going so damn fast
that any light we see is only light from in front, we're moving
too fast for it to catch up to us."

"You're a hostile apprentice," Richard grunted. "Okay,
here we go, you have the spar. Now, don't unfold it all at
once."

"Why not?" I asked.

"You don't know?" Richard mocked me by imitating my
unsure voice back at me.

I glared at him. "I wouldn't ask if I didn't."

"Because you seem to know so much already." He folded
his arms.

"Don't be such an ass," I said. "If I'm asking, I genuinely
want to know. What can't I open up full throttle right away?"

He leaned forward, hands on his knees in his harness,
tubes tapping the sides of his chair. "These cosmic winds
flitting past at superluminal speeds will hit the contact points of
the spar. It's filled with exotic matter that can clutch with the
wind. Drop a spar, it'll just rip free of the ship. There isn't a
tough enough substance to handle that impact. And if there
was, would you really think going from zero to faster than light
in a few seconds would be good for you? Human flavored jam
might be a rumored delicacy to the Kai Hanimar, but I don't
want to end being paste. Do you?"

Right. Entertainment always showed captains shouting
'full spar' and ships snapping into a sort of bristle, and then
zooming off into the wine dark sky.

But it wasn't like that, was it?

"Okay, how do I do it right?"

Richard clapped his hands together, and pulled them
slowly apart, leaving a small model of a sparship in the air. He
wiggled his fingertips, and wind blew past it.

"Drop the tips of the spars out, just a tiny bit," he said, "to create turbulence. The bubble of that turbulence surrounds the ship, creating a safe zone. It is a tiny universe. It is *that* bubble you weave around the ship that then is struck by the wind, and carries you with it. That's why accelerating to faster than light doesn't kill us all. There is some leakage, which is why the whole ship feels like we're accelerating. We have to keep readjusting the turbulence."

That wasn't quite what I'd always thought. I'd always thought the spars dipped into a powerful stream and slingshotted the ship along.

It was more complicated.

"Okay," I said.

"The larger the bubble you create, the faster we go. Vary the nature of the streamers, and you can reach out and snag cross currents, ride over eddies and whirlpools, weather cross-storms. Are you ready to deploy your spar, Jane Hawkins?"

I was. So. Very. Ready.

"I'll be the captain of this simulation," Richard said. He pointed at one of the displays. "My commands are going to be on your board in three, two, one…"

DEPLOY SPARS, Richard ordered wordlessly. The command thrilled down my spine. He and I weren't one mind, but this was far more… intimate than just text, voice, or anything else I'd ever experienced. There was a compulsion hanging in the air.

I remembered Villem commanding me in the tiny room of the Inn when he'd infected me with the neural upgrades.

He'd been giving me captain's commands.

It was this shared neural space that allowed Argyros to split himself across various machines. And Villem through his spiders. And Richard and me to control the simulation together.

DEPLOY SPARS.

Superfast, and with vibratory anticipation, I edged my spar out into the wind. All throughout the virtual ship the other spars moved with me.

The edge of it struck the wind, and the entire board turned red. Alarms sounded. I moved to correct, but a wretched, sickening screech of metal split my eardrums. Explosions wracked the hull as pieces of my spar ripped free and bounced on down the hull, striking other spars.

Our simulated ship spun rapidly in circles, a temporary and faint bubble evaporating as debris flew everywhere.

"Shit." The simulation faded away. I was back in the niche across from Richard in the *Dorado*'s peeling corridors. "What happened?"

"You destroyed your first sparship," Richard said, not unkindly. "We all do. There's no beginner's luck on this. Our job isn't easy. Did you think you were special? That you would just master what takes everyone else so long?"

It had all happened so damn fast.

"Jane," Argyros's familiar voice said, startling me. I turned around in the jump seat and realized that all three of Argyros had been watching the whole thing. For a moment I was sure he'd figured out I'd stolen the meat. But he smiled at me. "It's an art and a craft. You get better the more you try."

I sank back a bit. "Did you come for me?"

"No," Argyros said. "Was hoping to talk to Richard. Give him the news that Mr. Arrow has died and that some of the sparmen will need to add Mr. Arrow's duties to theirs, sadly."

"Dead?" I said, shocked. "What happened?"

"We found him in his niche. Still plugged in. Burned himself out in his harness," Argyros said. "I think he unbalanced, trying to make sure he was performing at his tip-top. His neural setup was a bit old, he was trying too hard to compensate."

I thought about that, soberly. Thought about how fast that spar ripped away from me. How fast would I need to be to handle it? What would I need to do to myself to get my brain to handle minute changes on a picosecond level?

Arrow worked there. It just killed him. Villem had been a husk of a man. I thought about all those burned out riggers I'd seen passing through Sargasso.

"His funeral will be tomorrow morning," Argyros said. "A ship-wide service. For those not on spars, that is."

Chapter Eighteen

Over the next week and a half I became obsessed with the simulator. Argyros kept me fed with my favorite meals, and I had to frequently check in on the bridge to make sure the navigation and map synched up.

But here, on the *Dorado*, I was treated by the riggers like I was my own person and I gloried in it. No one nagged me, told me what to eat or wear, or when I should be asleep. In fact, since the entire ship had watches, there was always someone awake.

Argyros took me under his wing, a gentle and patient mentor. Though he couldn't manage a spar anymore, he had plenty of tips for me, culled from his own days of being in the Consensus.

I'd begged Richard to give me a registered copy of the simulator after he'd watched me destroy my virtual ship too many times and tired of my questions.

I'd tossed everything I'd packed against the walls of the tiny cabin. I didn't bother cleaning it up, just made nest out of the clothes and sat with my legs folded, working on trying to get the damn ship just to move.

I could never give this all up, I realized. I had to become a rigger. This was the life I had always dreamed of.

"I can't help out," Richard said when I cornered him in the galley after my three hundredth destroyed spar. "I'm running around picking up Arrow's responsibilities."

"Just one," I pleaded. "I think I'm getting close."

Richard grinned pointed steel. "It took me a month."

I set my jaw. "I think I'm getting close."

"Some things take a long time to master," Richard said. "You can't—"

"Close," I repeated.

"I'm in a hurry, I really need to be somewhere." He

shook his head and walked off. I stared at his back and growled with frustration.

The growling gave me an idea.

I dug the scarf out of the messy pile in my room, wrapped it around my neck, and hurried down to cargo hold twelve. I slipped in through the door, and activated the scarf with a quick swipe.

If I kept quiet, and skirted well clear of the tiger's enclosure, I figured I would be able to get in and out quickly enough. I could offer Richard another couple pounds of raw meat in exchange for some tutoring.

And if Richard wasn't interested, then maybe there were others on board who had the same odd fascination with the stuff.

At the cube I paused.

The sound of voices echoed off the walls around the hold as the door clanged shut behind others who'd joined me in the hold.

Crap!

I froze in place as I watched Argyros and two riggers walk toward the tiger's enclosure. I was right in their line of sight. They stopped on the outer cubes and leaned against them.

The tiger jumped on top of the cubes and then down to join them. Argyros tossed it a treat and rubbed its ears.

I did my best to imitate a statue.

More riggers wandered into the hold until I realized that, other than the sparmen on duty, most of the crew had gathered around Argyros.

Strange, I hadn't gotten any notice about a meeting. And neither Woodgrove, Dr. Armstrong, or the captain were here when Argyros held three right hands up into the air for attention and the natural hum of conversation stopped.

I almost stepped forward, still thinking this was some sort of all-hands meeting that I'd forgotten about.

But then Argyros started talking.

"I know some of you only by your reputation scores," he

began. "But you all come loaded high and with good references, even if the names you used to get aboard this ship were fake."

He smiled, and I thought... fake?

What was with that smile. It made me shiver.

"The rest of you, you already know me from our time aboard the *SparkFlint*. The ship were I was torn apart in battle and left like you see me here, unable to join you all on the spars."

I almost shifted, shocked by hearing that. *Argyros*? On the *SparkFlint*? The ship from my childhood's tall tales. The menace?

"When the Kai Hanimar threatened our ships, laid in wait around planets, when they shoved us clear back to the point people were worried they would appear around Earth and destroy us, it was folk like me that laid down our resources to help equip and arm ships to take the fight *back out there*," Argyros said, his voice bitter. "There was no Grand Distributed Navy, like today. Just *us*. Riggers. Standing there on the edge of known space and spitting right back at those slimy tentacled aliens.

"We risked life and fortune to beat the Kai Hanimar back past Gliese, to secure a place for ourselves in the stars. But what happened after the war?"

"Nothing," shouted one of the older riggers, a wizened tiny man who wore a gleaming, powered exoskeleton scrimshawed with solar maps and alien cartoglyphs.

"Nothing," Argyros said. "They decommissioned our ships, and took away our right to remain armed. After what the Kai Hanimar did to us in the beginning, those ground-side bureaucrats stripped us of our right to defend ourselves out there in the naked cold of space."

General angry mutters mirrored Argyros's angry words back at him.

Agyros held up a hand to quiet everyone again. His human hand alone. "Even worse, they refused to compensate us for investments made. We won a war, and came back to nothing. So some of us refused to disarm and come in. We kept on hitting the Kai Hanimar, and for that they called us terrorists. Terrorists? I've been aboard a ship that the Kai Hanimar raided. I still dream about the things they did to those men. Some things you can't unsee. We ripped into those damn octopus-looking things.

"Then we started going after the traders working with the Kai Hanimar. Most of those trade companies, they didn't get involved during the war. Didn't help us up-armor ships, or get them armed. Just waited out the war. So we started hitting them. Gave them a taste of the troubles we suffered. And after all that, it came down to the standoff between the Distributed Navy and *SparkFlint*'s fleet."

"And they won," said Richard Johnson. I had to force myself not to be upset and shuffle when I saw him smile as Argyros glowered back at him. "You can lecture us all about time's past, Argyros, but none of us here are going back to war. We signed up for a share of the *SparkFlint*'s treasure, not to repeat old battles."

Argyros deflated a bit, and his eyes narrowed. "I know they won. I wake up every day knowing they won. I'm not asking for a repeat. But what I do want to do is contextualize what we're doing here: we're going to become enemies of the Navy again. Outcasts."

"But we'll be rich as hell," laughed the man in the exoskeleton.

"And most of you will squander it trying to run a ship of your own because you'll no longer be able to crew aboard anything," Argyros said. "I created the Spyglass as a haven in a hostile place for just us riggers. To try and help us have a place of our own in Canaveral. I sold it to a bunch of posers. With that money, and once I have my share of this venture, I'm going to disappear."

"How?" asked one of the riggers. Colorado Jones, I saw, risking checking his public handle. He was a stellar cartographer, a navigator that worked closely with the captain.

Yet, I had just learned that none of the crew was who we

thought. Who was Colorado Jones really?

"That's none of your business," said Argyros.

"Fair enough," said Colorado. "The captain has the final route laid in, we're on approach. I know the destination well enough. So I guess it's time we talked about what we do with the crew once we've taken the ship for ourselves."

"The captain is a good at handling the ship," Argyros said. "And you all know it. Best to wait until we're on our way back before we hijack her."

And there it was, in the open. The word hijack seemed to fall out of the air and into the space between the riggers.

"After all," Argyros said. "While you're all shareholders in this venture that, and remember this, *I* put together and recruited most of you for, what happens once we have the ship? Will the sparsmen discipline of the captain's current crew be here to help us remain in line? No. It's a good chance your overclocked, jumpy selves will start creating feedback loops while on the spars. What a shame it would be to gain the treasure of a lifetime just to rip our own ship apart on the way out. Some of you think you're better than human because of all your upgrades, and that you can handle anything. But you're as liable to kill us as anything."

"You're a real ass, Argyros," Richard said, folding his arms.

"And you're not the CEO of this little venture," said Colorado Jones. "We're riggers. We have to have a consensus. You can whip the vote, and negotiate between conflicts, but right now, most of us feel pretty similar. We should take the ship now."

"Then call the consensus," Argyros said. "We are one, as sparsmen, or nothing at all. I don't disagree with that." The words sounded rehearsed, as if a motto.

The riggers held up their hands, and in the center of the virtual space between a digital representation of a black maelstrom began to swirl and coalesce, long fingers of black reaching down through the air to stab at each of the men.

The neural integration their implants gave them was

being used to create a shared computing space.

I knew this was what they did when riding the spars. Creating a melded overmind that could handle the greater task of flying a sparship at superhuman speeds. Now they were creating a temporary version of that to come to some sort of decision.

And I recognized the swirl.

A physical version of it had crawled up Villem Osteonidus's arm and tried to force him to walk down to the group of riggers calling out to him.

"It's settled," Colorado said to Argyros, and the sound of their voices again after the long intense silence of their communing battered at me. "We take the ship."

"I offer an amendment," Argyros said, looking weary.

"What, maroon them on some tiny, out of the way planet with no equipment to salve your morality? You know that's just as much a death sentence as anything else we'll do."

"No," Argyros said. "I'll abide by the consensus here. But we should wipe their minds with a neural surge. Turn Woodgrove and her crew into vegetables. It gives us an alibi that simple disappearance doesn't if we get caught, or questioned. We say they were playing at being riggers, and got caught in a bad eddy."

"The captain?"

Argyros smiled coldly. "He tried to save their lives. Look, Richard, you've been helping the girl log hours on a simulator. Those are credentialed. We can use the authentication keys as proof they were meddling where they shouldn't."

I bit my lip. All along he'd been setting me up. I'd be the one blamed to have accidentally killed Lady Woodgrove, Doctor Armstrong, and myself.

And maybe even any crew that weren't a part of this plot.

They were going to kill me.

That fear that had dwelled in me back at the inn, that I thought I'd left far, far behind, returned.

And still, through all this, I'd remained absolutely still. Despite the sweat trickling down the small of my back. Despite the tremors starting to develop in the back of my legs from standing right here, listening to everything.

How much longer could my body stand this?

The *Dorado* shook and shivered. Spars realigned and grabbed unseen currents, energies collided and very slowly filtered through into the bubble around the ship.

We were being yanked down out of faster than light speeds.

Argyros looked around. "We're here."

Colorado Jones nodded. "You'll coordinate the taking of the ship, Argyros. We're agreed. We had a consensus."

Argyros nodded. "I will make the call. But I will wait for the right moment. Once they lead us to what we want. Understand? I won't have *anyone* screw that up."

He glared danger and violence, daring anyone to respond.

"Understood," Richard murmured, looking down at the ground.

Chapter Nineteen

The moment the riggers all left the room I let out the longest breath and sat down to rub my legs and shake out my arms.

PIECES OF MEAT? Argyros's tiger asked hopefully when it saw me running by, but I ignored it to creep out of the hold.

An invitation appeared in the ship's public space. An envelope in the upper right corner of my vision as I walked along the dripping, groaning corridors of the ship's innards.

FROM: Cpt. Garrik.

"I welcome all crew to the ship's cockpit," his voice said when I selected the note. "From here we will enjoy the tradition of planetfall and celebrate the launch of our real mission. The Lady Woodgrove has planned a special feast and will update you all on your roles in the exploration teams."

I waved the invitation away.

Service robots crammed the hallways bearing trays of snacks and drinks expertly on gimbaled trays, creating a long train all the way to the cockpit. Argyros stood in their midst with a grin, directing them.

"Planetfall!" he shouted at me as I ran past toward the bridge. I'd been hoping to slip by. I didn't think I could look at him without freaking out and him realizing, somehow, that I *knew* what was happening.

One of his metal selves grabbed my shoulder in a cheerful side-hug.

"It is always a good day when you fall out of lightspeed and into a planet's orbit. No matter what else is swirling around, we always take a moment to relish the fact that we survived. The first ships did not always make it." Argyros handed me a cup of bright red punch.

I sipped it, trying not to spill it as the robotic servers, Argyros, and I all streamed toward the cockpit.

The punch had kick. Had I gotten rum punch by mistake? When I looked at Argyros in surprise he put a finger to his lips.

"Tell no one," he winked. "Enjoy the adventure! I remember my first planetfall. My first mission! You'll see amazing things, Jane. Amazing things!"

And I was swept into the cockpit.

Lady Woodgrove looked so thrilled her cheeks had gotten rosy. She'd changed into a dramatic-looking black dress with a high collar and what looked like millions of dollars in diamonds draped in a net across her chest. Her eyes glittered when she saw me.

"Jane Hawkins," she pronounced as she swept over. "We have arrived."

"Lady Woodgrove, I need to talk to you," I muttered, trying not to be conspicuous. There were riggers crowding in. All around me were fanned heads, coolant-tentacles slapping, tattoos springing through the air. Steel and plumage and stapled-shut eyes.

"Oh Jane, we will talk. We will talk," Woodgrove promised, and sashayed away to excitedly babble to a massive, overly-muscled rigger.

I snarled to myself. That woman was lost in a high of her own excitement.

But then, so was Doctor Armstrong. He waved cheerily at me, and then walked right over to Argyros to sample whatever exotic little tidbits were on the silver platters.

Alarms chirped throughout the ship, the bird-like sounds echoing off the walls. The *Dorado* vibrated, more spars gripping that unseen current around us.

I felt my stomach lift from the unsettling feeling of weightlessness. We weren't accelerating inside of our bubble of space and energy anymore. We had come to a stop. And that meant we were adrift in space.

We were really near our location.

Shielded blast windows shivered aside on hardened rails, and the sight of normal, open space ahead grabbed my attention. This was the real. Naked reality. Unadorned. Seen through thick transparent metal windows all around the cockpit and not just screens on the walls.

"What is this place?" Doctor Armstrong asked loudly.

Even though I'd seen glimpses of our destination before in my own head, I still stared out at the field of boulders ahead. They clustered tightly together in a mist of dust. Behind them, a startlingly blue-banded gas giant dominated the sky. It felt like we were falling in toward the edge of its cerulean atmosphere, and the odd blue light of it filled the cockpit with strange hues and shadows.

"The boneyard," Argyros said softly, staring at the tight clump of rocks and dust. We were all quiet enough to hear the squeak of the robotic servers and tink of glasses, so his words were clear to us. "This is the *SparkFlint*'s refuge. It built all this, moving all these rocks together, burrowing equipment into them. It died right here after the battle of Fagin Sound."

Ah, I thought. This was how I could reveal him for who he was in front of Woodgrove and the others.

"So you've seen this place before?" I asked, a little louder than I had intended. That drink Argyros gave me was messing with my thinking a little.

He looked over at me. "I'm a rigger, Jane. We've seen some media of the old ship's exploits. Many of us know a friend who knows a friend who once served on the ship. But, I can happily say I've never seen this place myself before now."

I wanted to belligerently challenge what I assumed was a bold, smooth lie. But then I saw all those blank riggers' faces looking at me, and let it drop.

My rum punch wobbled off into the air away from me, pieces of the drink breaking off into bubbles in the middle of the air by my nose.

Right. Weightlessness. I started trying to shoo the pieces of punch back into the cup, but only ended up breaking it into smaller and smaller pieces of floating liquid.

A tiny robot, like a fat wasp, zipped through the air and gulped up the punch. Within a second the air was clean again.

"Trigger the lid," a nearby rigger said, laughing as he

noticed my fumbling around. "The button's on the bottom."

When I did that, a cover snicked in from the thick rim of the glass and sealed the top.

"And figure out how to use your deck shoes," he also added, as I was wobbling unsteadily in the air myself.

He left to join the others crowding the platters of food as Woodgrove and Argyros together jostled people and encouraged them to eat and celebrate. I remained in place, trying to figure out how to trigger the electromagnets in my shoes so that I could stick myself to the floor.

With practice, riggers could trigger the magnets without even thinking about it as they moved around, 'walking' through the ship if they needed to. Though most choose to fly through the corridors and whip around the air. It was faster that way for them.

Long after the riggers got bored of looking out over the boneyard Captain Garrik stood there, looking out in the haze.

He stood far enough apart from everyone I could move to stand next to him, shuffling my way over with deck shoes as casually as I could for a first time user.

"Captain," I whispered. "Argyros plans to take over the ship. He's got most of the riggers on his side."

Captain Garrik didn't move. He kept staring at the boneyard. "How do you know?" he asked, and pointed out a large, misshapen and pock-marked orb. The largest planetoid in the strange cloud ahead of us. As if he were talking to me about it.

Without even thinking about it, something inside me focused on it and my vision cleared everything around me away. *Thanatos*, said a tag. I scrunched my face and willed it all to go away. I had bigger things to focus on than the name of the giant rock.

I told the captain everything. About my scarf spoofing virtual sight. And the tiger in the hold. As I described the meeting, his back stiffened, and his jaw clenched slightly.

Contained anger rolled off him for a split second, and then faded as he controlled himself. "They knowingly joined me in the consensus-space of the ship while we flew," he said. "I shared neural space with those pieces of shit, and they plan to take the ship. *Assholes*. I should throw the spars open and rip the hull to shreds. Leave them stranded."

Then he sighed, and rubbed his forehead. "I'm sorry. I think, on some deeper level, I knew something was wrong. A certain, off kind of feeling. And, as of fifteen minutes ago, my security programs started alerting me to something sniffing its way through the ship's systems. They need me alive and connected to the ship for now, they're trying to lift my authentication keys. That'll take a while. And they won't want to really move until we're going after the trove that you directed us to. They'll keep their pretense up until they have one or the other."

"So what do we do?" I asked.

"I have enough supplies to stock up a skip ship without being noticed," Captain Garrik muttered. "Including weapons. We can make a run for it with crew I trust and hide in the Boneyard somewhere while I signal for help, or we could hold up in the ship's engineering core. Until then, we do nothing. Reveal nothing."

"Nothing?"

"You are young. Do people often underestimate you?" Garrik asked.

I looked over at him. He seemed taller than me all the other times I'd seen him: standing ramrod straight, in command of the room. Now I realized he was only a couple inches taller.

"Yes," I said, thinking about the small slights and assumptions made about the girl working at the desk, or cleaning up after breakfast.

"It's a weapon you and I both have right now. Probably our only one," he said softly. "If it gets really bad, Jane, see if you can mingle with Argyros's crew. It might buy you some more time."

"Pretend to join them?" I was outraged at his suggestion that I lie and join the plotting riggers. "They wanted to kill me for the map back on Sargasso."

"You delay and lead them where they want to go. Play for time. They won't risk losing access to the map by ripping it from you if they can get you to just help them. Argyros would rather kill you later than make things harder right away. There is a level-headed practicality about him. And, remember, time is its own win, Jane. Sometimes just surviving opens other avenues, it gives chance time to give you an opportunity."

I wasn't sure I believed that. Argyros was a dangerous man who planned on murdering me and my friends. Surviving with his help didn't sound *right*. But I swallowed that objection. "Okay."

Captain Garrik spread his arms. "Stay alive, Jane. I'll contact you when my plans are ready for us to make a move. Too soon and they will be able to overwhelm us. I only trust four of my crew on the spars right now. I know for sure they served in the Navy. That means there are nineteen of Argyros's people against us. We need to get this just right. All the ship's a stage, now, Jane. Play your part."

My mouth dry, I nodded.

Nineteen dangerous riggers were planning to kill us. On our side: four crew the captain felt he could trust, plus Woodgrove and Doctor Armstrong.

And me?

Chapter Twenty

I wanted to spend the next few hours brooding in my room. But I had this gnawing worry that it would make me look guilty of something. And, even though Agyros had no idea I'd overheard him and the other riggers, it still felt like hiding myself away would look suspicious.

In the main hold, the rainbow and steel-colored riggers gently guided crates through the middle of the air into crab-like pods that could squirt away from the *Dorado* to go explore the boneyard. Two riggers hung upside down in the air next to a pod. They welded extra sensors and equipment on, the crack and sizzle of their welders echoed around the bay as sparks spit and danced in the air.

The captain had long ago deemed docking with Thanatos to be too risky. So half the crew went down with the skips and the other half stayed.

Most of the riggers ignored me. Electric excitement snapped and roiled around the room like silent lightning. The normally moody and focused riggers grinned at each other, exchanging sly conspiratorial looks as they geared up.

Argyros stood in the bay, surrounded by the machines, no such smile on his lips.

"Jane." He nodded at me as I carefully and deliberately walked around a ten-foot-high drillbit held in the oversized mechanical claws of one of the pods.

The *Dorado* shook and shivered as old chemical rockets nudged the ship in closer in between the rock field.

"They don't look all that large when you're in the cockpit," Argyros said. "But each of those rocks is the size of a small skyscraper. You could lose yourself in each one. Without a map."

I looked at him, and forced myself to smile. "I guess that's me," I said in a slightly chipper voice.

Argyros's smile looked shark-like, illuminated in jumping shadows by the bright, random light of the welder in the bay. "I guess it is, Jane."

I mumbled an excuse about pressure and hid behind a pod to get control of myself. Standing that close to Argyros had left me visibly nervous. I needed to regain my personal calm.

Someone grabbed my shoulder.

I spun around and punched them right in the chest. The rigger Joyce Bandu flew away from me, her arms flailing. Her purple mohawk sparkled in the twinkling welding-lit light of the hold.

"Damn it, kid," she shouted as she spun herself around, hit the wall on her feet, and pushed gently back off toward me.

Standing next to where she *had* been, Red Ruth was laughing and taking a step back away with the little 'click' that deck shoes made.

Red snagged Joyce out of the air and let her re-anchor herself to the floor. "Captain sent us over here," she said. She wore a bright red lab-leather jacket and her ruby red, artificial eyes glowed demonically as she smiled. "We're going to be your bodyguards. We're armed. Bandu here spent time working security details and has training. I've also worked as a captain's personal bodyguard."

I shook my head. "No. I've looked around this hold. Most of Argyros's men want to go down into the boneyard. He's leaving just a handful behind. Anyone who comes with me is someone who can't stay behind to fight to regain the ship. I won't be responsible for that."

Joyce raised an eyebrow, her anger suddenly vaporized. "That's noble of you, Jane. But we can't abandon you to these skeevy bastards down there."

"You have to," I insisted. "If you don't hold the ship, then it's all for nothing. We're dead. You know this."

Red stepped forward. "We know that. But it's not guaranteed that we can take the ship. You should still have someone with you. Joyce will stay."

"That's still…"

"I'm not negotiating," Red snapped. "I'm telling you how it's going to go."

I swore under my breath. "Okay."

Argyros's voice filled the bay as he ordered, "Load up!"

The crack of authority in his voice was clear to anyone in the bay.

He was in charge of the riggers.

The crew dove into pods and skip ships. I crawled into the nearest skip, a narrow tube with a blistered and blackened old chemical rocket fused to the back. As I strapped in with the other riggers, one of Argyros's robots peered in.

"That you in there, Jane?"

I leaned forward against the crude straps.

"I'm here," I said with gritted teeth. The nervousness kicked in again. We were really doing this. Jumping out of the ship and into the boneyard. Into the *SparkFlint*'s refuge. I could feel sweat on the bridge of my nose.

The shiny face nodded approval. There was excitement in the audio, though the rigid, blank face didn't emote anything.

"Good," Argyros said, and shut the door.

The clank and hiss made me shiver. I was locked in with the riggers. The pilot of the skip glanced back at me.

"Let's get rich," he grinned.

On a set of dirty, old wall-mounted screens I watched the bay doors jerk open now that the floors were clear of people. Air and water vapor blew out in a sparkling cloud, and then the pods and skips all squirted out into the darkness of open space, racing for the large, potato-shaped lump of rock in space called Thanatos.

We were tiny specks of metal, glinting in the gas planet's strong light, approaching what had once been an asteroid. The *SparkFlint* had towed it here, along with other space debris to be mined and turned into a base of operations.

It was freaking huge, I thought, now that we hurtled along its shadow. It spun slowly on the longer axis, forcing us to approach it by one of the ends.

I was expecting small airlocks, or something. But, as we

approached, massive doors on the end-caps of Thanatos slowly rolled aside.

"The old codes still work," someone whispered loudly.

The skip floated into the core through the doors of the giants. Smoothly bored-out rock walls slipped past us, lit up by large spotlights on the skip's hull.

Behind us, the doors quietly blocked out the stars as they sealed themselves back shut.

The pilot passed the skip through another set of giant doors that now opened. A hundred-foot-tall grinning skull looked down at us, the visage etched into the front of the doors by lasers long ago. Not a positive omen of things to come, I thought.

A dim, ghastly light filled the interior of Thanatos, filtered down from the other end-cap on the far end. That end was transparent, and pointed toward the gas giant we all orbited.

The entire inside of Thanatos had been hollowed out. Maybe by the *SparkFlint*'s star-bright lasers themselves. The curved insider of the tube-shaped interior of Thanatos was covered in gray dirt, and scattered across the dirt was overgrown jungle. The entire thing was an abandoned botanical garden.

Below me, I could see a swamp, surrounded by humanoid statues covered in moss.

There was a landing pad ringed by rocks.

We hung in the air like hummingbirds once we'd emerged from the end-cap's massive airlock. Then the skips fired their engines and lowered themselves carefully to the 'ground.' We were really stuck against the inside of the spinning asteroid, but as we lowered ourselves to the wall and moved away from the middle of the carved out asteroid's center, I could feel gravity return.

It was not a gravity as heavy as Earth's, or the press when the *Dorado* accelerated. But I gratefully welcomed the return a sense of weight, and the notion of up and down.

Dust kicked up into the air as the skip settled to the ground, rockets underneath me shuddering and kicking me in the rear as the skip slowed down.

A silver-eyed rigger by the gullwing door of the skip announced that the air outside was okay for us to breathe without assistance, then opened the door. My ears popped as air rushed out of the skip. They were pressurized differently.

The stale, metallic smell of the skip was invaded by what smelled like humid, rotten eggs from the outside. It was the smell of a failed ecosystem. Soggy plants and creepers, stagnant water.

And yet, I was aware that I was standing on the inside of a giant can made out of rock, spinning so that it created enough force for me to stick to the inside as if it were the surface of a world.

On all sides of me, stretching up and then overhead, more land. More gray and green swamp and jungle, fetid lakes, and even irregular hills.

It felt like standing amongst the ruins of some great, overgrown lost empire.

"Come on," Red said, walking away from another group of disembarking riggers. Her red eyes and jacket looked darker and more menacing in the eerie light, though I did see, far overhead, some large rectangles of pure brightness. Large lighting panels. Though most of them were dark and no longer working.

Riggers watched us move to the side of the landing pad, and its decorative boulders. I could tell Red was forcing me away from them.

"Now's the time," she hissed.

"Time?"

"To run. You have an entire worldlet here to hide in, Hawkins. Get cracking. Stay clear of Argyros, and get somewhere where Captain Garrick can pick you up once he has control of the ship. You helped lure them off the ship. Now run."

"But..."

"I'll be off to 'join' them, as I've been the clueless crew up until now. I'll distract. But I'll be okay. *Now get out of here.*"

I hadn't even had time to orient myself. I'd seen the ring of boulders around the landing space. I knew there was a hill, and a large stone building nearby. And lots of jungle and swamp-looking areas.

But Red Ruth was right. I'd gotten here. Garrick, Armstrong and Woodgrove would be fighting for their ship. I'd done my part.

Now it was time to run.

But there were riggers landing further out around the clearing. They were fanning out.

I would be spotted.

I ducked around behind one of the boulders. I pulled out my scarf and wrapped it around my neck, fingered the controls, and triggered the electronics that would hack shared vision and hide me from their eyes.

Now I had to wait for the right moment to slip away.

Chapter Twenty-One

Forcing myself to calmly stand with my back against the cold rock of the boulder was actually welcome. I had time just to glance around, though I couldn't move my head or I would give myself away.

I watched Red stalk her way back to the other riggers after she looked around, puzzled at my sudden dissapearance. Captain Garrick hadn't told her *everything* about me, it seemed.

Argyros detached himself from a small council of men, though one of his robotic selves remained with them, and approached Red.

"Red Ruth!" he exclaimed, friendly and welcoming. He reached out to shake her hand.

Red folded her arms. "What are you offering, Argyros?"

She wasn't making a large scene, but everyone watched her. Red had a presence that got attention. Even among riggers.

"You're direct," Argyros said. "I appreciate that. Like I said aboard the skip on the way in, we're here to make ourselves rich. No one is interested in fighting. We're trying to leave that far behind us, my crew has seen all too much of that in the past."

"*Your* crew?" Red asked.

And there it all was, out in the open. No alluding to this, or suggesting that, as I imagined Argyros had been doing before. The cloying, honest truth had descended upon the open pad.

Argyros spread the arms of his metal self on the left. The other body standing with the riggers turned around, now, to watch Red rather intensely. The human piece of Argyros stepped forward. "Yes. *My* crew," he said softly. "Not Garrick's. Not anyone else's. Mine, because we spilled blood together. Because we bonded in shared space while riding the spars together."

Red shifted from foot to foot, nervous. "Look. I put my reputational score and resume on the line every time I join a crew. I can't spit all over a lifetime of work. You're a powerful man, Argyros. I'd be a fool to ignore that. But I've been a rigger as long as any here, I'm not some fleshy newcomer, I'm as glinty as they come. I don't know what we're going to discover here, or if there really is a trove of wealth waiting for us here, and I am certainly not going to stake my life's work on a story that—"

She was cut off by the sound of a gunshot and a scream. I twitched in place, filled with a sudden horror at the fact that I had moved. But no one looked my way, everyone had turned in the direction of the loud crack.

Argyros didn't turn, or flinch. His three selves stared at Red Ruth with all the friendliness of a swaying cobra.

Red looked back at his human face, her mouth compressed into a tight line. "What was that, Argyros?"

"That was Alan," Argyros said, his voice cold, like metal. "He, apparently, did not want to join. Well, he said he did. But when he got into the consensus and joined our shared neural space, it turned out he was clearly lying."

Red Ruth looked around at all the riggers, then back at Argyros. I expected her to run, or to fight back. But she'd looked around at the numbers and come to some sort of decision.

She straightened her back. "Mr. Argyros, I'm going back to the ship. You know me, and my reputation. I'm being straightforward when I say I'm not going to cause you trouble in your hunt for the *SparkFlint*'s treasures. But I want out of this conflict. I'm a rigger. I want to ride the currents between the stars. That's it. You do what you must."

She turned her back to him and walked toward the pitted hull of one of the older skips.

That speech had sucked some of the tense air right out of the landing pad. There were other riggers who had nodded with her, respecting the sentiment. Red had known who she was speaking to. And what to say.

There walked a future captain, I thought.

And so did many of the other riggers, watching her walk by them. Something had shifted in the inter-group dynamic. Halfway to the skip, Argyros grunted. A frustrated and resigned sound. His two metal selves blurred as they ran, articulated feet making only a silent tapping sound as they crossed the space to Red.

I opened my mouth to shout a warning, but in the time it took for me to part my lips the two metallic bodies struck Red.

She gasped, struck in the small of her back, arching and flying forward.

The leftmost piece of Argyros grabbed Red by the skull and smashed it against the rocky floor of the landing area. Blood spattered across shiny, metalloid hands as both aspects of Argyros continued bashing her head in.

Only the whining sound of robotic movements trickled through the air as I shivered and took a step back, breaking free of the rock. I was risking being seen, but I was shaking with shock. I'd seen fighting. I'd seen death, had someone taken from me.

I'd even known this was possible, but seeing it shook me.

I knew I couldn't unsee this. This horrific, violent act. Red Ruth had been a captain-in-waiting. We could all see it. She'd been noble.

She'd been speaking to us all, just a few minutes ago.

Now she was gone. Absent. Her body still. Empty.

Argyros's human body walked over and looked down at the bloodied, dead Ruth sprawled in front of him. His two other selves straightened.

He took out a cloth from his pocket and carefully cleaned their hands.

I turned and ran, understanding how real this all was. Argyros was a murderer. His crew had just stood there and watched it. I understood now, deep down to the pit of my stomach, that I would die by the hands of these riggers if I stayed.

There was no going back. No rejoining his crew and

pretending anything. Red had been right, I thought, wiping at a tear in the corner of my eye. I had to run now, and evade them, and hope I could get picked up by the captain and Woodgrove once they got the ship back.

If they got the ship back.

Maybe I could figure out how to survive inside Thanatos. There had to be stores somewhere. Or trees that grew food. I could hide until the murdering riggers left. Because just staying alive was maybe all I could hope for.

Better to starve or struggle than have my head bashed in.

I trudged through swamp and muck, my shoes filling with mud and nastiness, thorny vines and bushes brushing at my calves. On overly large insect buzzed by me.

The longer I ran, the further away I got from Argyros.

Covered in silt, my own breath hot in my cut and bleeding face, I didn't stop until the light faded. I'd run deep into the heart of Thanatos, under a patch of the inside where those large lights had guttered out.

Tall pine trees filtered out the distant light of the gas giant. I walked through skeins of indigo shadows, as if underwater, surrounded by green dust mites.

I caught my breath as I stood in place, grateful to be alive, my thighs and calves set on fire with pain.

Something stirred behind one of the trees.

A pine needle cracked under a foot.

I held my breath, my heart leaping. Absolutely still, and hopefully invisible, I waited as a shadow shifted from between the blue-gray trunks of the pines.

Chapter Twenty-Two

The shadow between the trees stopped.

"I see you," it said.

The voice was only partly human. The rest was a sub-electronic gargle. The virtual air around me dimmed and spat static.

For a moment I thought about running again. Turning back where I came from. But the thought of Agyros calmly wiping the blood from his metallic fingers stopped me.

"You deploy visual counter-measures," the voice said. "But I can see you."

"Step forward and show yourself," I ordered with more authority than I ever dreamed I had. My knees shivered with fear, but I stood straight.

"I'm designed to spot ghosts like you," the mechanical-human voice grated, and the shadow stepped forward.

A Frankenstein's monster of a mess stood in the trees. The remains of what had once been a man. Shredded skin melted into patches of chitinous polycarbon, and chunks of him were just plain missing.

I saw ribcage exposed, and underneath that transparent ports, metal organs twisting away inside. A red light gleamed near the spine, pulsing like a heart.

It had no hands. Tools snapped and whirred into place as it gestured at me. Manipulators, welders, data ports, knives, guns.

"Are you real?" the monster asked.

An artificial eye whirred and focused on me, and superconductor ports dangled from the center of a shaved skull as it took another step closer and I tried not to scream.

"I'm real," I said, in the strongest voice I could muster. "I'm Jane Hawkins."

"Jane Hawkins!" the monster said, as if that meant

something very profound to it. "Jane Hawkins! Well, well. I'm so pleased to meet you. What a tremendous moment. A tremendous moment. A tremendous moment."

After repeating itself it grew confused for a second and looked around.

"I'm Jane Hawkins?" I said, again. "And who are you?"

A large barrel rolled and locked into place along the monster's left forearm. It caressed the curved metal with a right hand made of robotic fingers that made a 'tink' sound as they tapped the new device.

"Don't be scared: I am gun," the thing said. "And no one left any ammunition behind here, so I can't shoot you."

"I see," I said, although I really didn't. I took a step back from it.

"I am Weapon," it said. "Am I imagining you?"

It said that with a sort of sad longing. As if suspected I wasn't real, and that this sort of hallucination had happened to it before.

"I'm real," I said.

"They've said that before. But it's always a lie," the mess of machine and, now that I could see what stood clearly before me, man grumbled. "It's always misplaced memories, come back to haunt me. I was ripped apart, and I pieced myself back together from artillery nets and spare parts that I could inhabit. Sometimes I find pieces of memories scattered around. Sometimes it's just memories the other machines in here have of the past. The ghosts of the *Sparkflint*. The ghosts of my being trapped in this place alone for far too long."

I felt sad for the creature. Despite the knives and barrels and cameras, a broken person clung to life inside. He might look like a nightmare of a cyborg as imagined by someone with a weapons fetish, but it sounded ready to cry. I had to prove to it I was real, though. I couldn't just leave it think I was someone from its imagination.

At least it didn't seem interested in harming me.

So I lowered my shoulder and ran at it.

I collided with the transparent breast plate. A dull thud. I had expected to knock the thing back a bit, but instead I just bounced off it like I'd struck a wall.

Winded and gasping I staggered back, clutching my bruised shoulder.

But Weapon rose taller, as if straightening its back. "That was real," it said, the wistfulness in its voice lost. Artificial eyes and shoulder-mounted cameras both looked down at me with surprise and delight. "You *are* real."

Weapon laughed, a startling grating sound that caused large shimmering dragonflies to burst free of their hiding places in the low grass, their wings shimmering in the air.

"I am," I said. "I'm Jane. What do you want me to call you?"

It was the first of a lot of questions I had.

"I think, once upon a time, many years ago, I was called Ben. Oh, it's so nice to meet you! All these years, stranded here. Trying to keep myself together. And trying to build myself a way home. I think I was getting desperate enough to even try."

"Ben," I said. Ben the Gun. No, Ben the Weapon. "It's nice to meet you, too, Ben." He had to know a lot about Thanatos. And that would have to be useful.

If I was careful, I might find myself an ally.

Ben looked around. "But how did you get here?" He turned back around, and suspiciously asked. "Who are you here with? And *how* did you find Thanatos?"

I took a step back. This was the tricky bit, wasn't it?

Ben shuddered, and raised his hands. "Wait, I see it. Oh, so beautiful."

"You see what?"

Artificial eyes turned back to me. "Your ship," Ben said. "A real ship."

"The *Dorado*," I said. "You can see it? That's how we got here."

Metallic tendons snicked as the tree-trunk thick, carbon-fiber arms reached gingerly out to me. "I see many things, tapped into the systems here. But you must be careful, and quiet. In case you wake the vengeful ghosts of the past. That's how I've remained alive. Care. Careful, fastidious, care."

"Okay," I said, nodding to play along.

Satisfied I'd heeded the warning, Ben moved closer, filling the air between us with the smell of oil, decay, and hard metal.

"Who crews your ship, Jane? And do you think they would accept a passenger like me? Are they tolerant people? Because, I have a secret..."

"A secret?"

Even closer, metal and man creaked. "Get me out off this haunted shithole and I'll make you all richer than a corporate king. I will more than pay my way. I'll *change your life*."

I swallowed. I had heard those words before. And now, they didn't fill me with a sort of jittery hunger. Now they made me wince. "That might be a problem," I said. "There's been a mutiny."

Ben pulled back.

"Mutiny," he muttered. The word didn't seem to surprise him, but fill him with a soft sadness. "Ahh."

I explained everything briefly to him, ending with my leading the riggers down here, and then Red Ruth's death. Repeating that last bit made me almost want to throw up. I still couldn't swipe the image clean from the back of my head of the blood. On the ground, staining her jacket, pooling in the ground by her side.

"Clever to draw them down here," Ben mused.

"I'm less interested in treasure or riches," I said firmly. Ben hiccuped a slight laugh, which I ignored as I continued, "than in just getting home. I just want to go home again."

"Oh," Ben whispered with so much wistfulness in his voice that I felt an unasked for lump in my throat. "Home again. It has been so many years I've been marooned inside this rocky shell. You know what I miss most?"

I shook my head. "No?"

"Cheese," the cyborg said. "Toasted brie, in fact. With flat little crackers. Sharp cheddar melted over anything. Oh, a real gouda, smoked. With fresh grapes. That, I'm convinced, is a magical thing. There is no cheese here on Thanatos. Just protein algae. As much of that as the emergency survival machines produce. And then there are the canned and preserved things accidentally left by the old crew. I hunt their little signals. I had a can of beans a few weeks ago with tiny little bits of maple bacon."

His voice quivered as he mentioned the bacon.

I thought back to the end of journey celebration. "There's real cheese aboard the *Dorado*," I said.

Ben snapped to stare at me with all the attention of a dog at hunt. "Is there now," he said. "Precisely, what kind?"

"Um," my memory went all wobbly. "Yellow?"

"Most likely a cheddar of some sort," Ben said thoughtfully, creaking as he moved to lean against a tree. "I used to fear losing everything, but it turns out I was wrong."

"How were you wrong?" I asked.

"Losing everything is hard," Ben said. "But in a place like this, alone and stranded, there is nothing but time to obsess over what you have lost."

That filled me with an ache inside. I twitched slightly.

A loud boom overhead startled us both. The sound echoed slowly through the curved, gray and blue walls of Thanatos. Overhead one of the *Dorado*'s skips glinted in the blue light as it swerved through the air.

Another skip followed it. Explosions rocked the air, and then both craft wobbled and plunged down out of the center of Thanatos and toward the inside surface, just two miles away from where we stood.

Ben's eyes whirred as they zoomed in and tracked the craft.

A large plume of smoke erupted from the crash site. One of the skips had exploded.

"Who made it to the ground?" Ben asked me, turning back. "What's happening?"

"I don't know." I thought about Captain Garrik, and Lady Woodgrove, and then Dr. Armstrong, and hoped that they were okay.

And then I thought about what the man in front of me had experienced, and knew that I couldn't hide away on Thanatos and somehow hope to make a life. I did not want to end up like Ben the Weapon.

"We have to go see who that is, and if we can help," I said to Ben. "This is how you get your cheese, and more. This is how we can get you home."

"I doubt there's a home anymore for me," Ben said. "Too much will have changed. But cheese... am I willing to risk my life for cheese?"

I stared at the construct of man in front of me. The seconds ticked slowly by as I waited for a decision.

Then Ben sighed. "You said the riggers were from the *Sparkflint*, yes?"

"Yes," I nodded.

"Their leader; his mind, is it all in one body? Or scattered and rebuilt. Like mine?"

I took a deep breath. "He calls himself Johnathan Argyros."

I hadn't named him yet. Now it hung in the air between us. Something dangerous and unsettling.

Weapons rearranged themselves on Ben's forearms. Clicking into place. But it was a nervous tic. The man himself stepped back toward the pine tree he'd leaned against.

"Argyros. Same man. He did this to me."

"How?" I asked, shocked.

"Six of us helped store treasure on Thanatos, bringing it from hiding places and holds to this location. The *SparkFlint* gave us these orders. You have to understand, the ship itself, by then, had become the Captain of its Consensus. We all gave pieces of ourselves to it, and it created an identity through scans of our brains. When the six of us tried to come back aboard, the *SparkFlint* ordered Argyros to kill us. He was happy to follow the orders. I fought him, but he was always a faster man than me. And he didn't entirely kill me. Just left me for dead. Destroyed me. Stranded me here with the ghosts of all those who remain to haunt Thanatos."

"Are you not going to come with me, then?" I asked, seeing the terror in Ben's face.

Pistons in Ben's legs hissed as he took a half step forward, then back. Trying to make up his mind.

"I'll come with," he muttered. Barrels rolled away, and a long, gleaming blade slide out from the cupped end of his fingerless forearm. "Just for a chance to stick this right into old Johnny Argyros's left eye."

"Good," I said, with more conviction than I really felt. I had an ally.

Chapter Twenty-Three

For a giant machine man, Ben was remarkably delicate in the woods. He brushed past the trees without making a sound, a blueish metal ghost moving from shadow to shadow.

We stopped at the edge of the crash site. The skip's belly had been mangled, but the rest of it looked okay. What looked like three foot high metal trash cans sat on each edge of the crash site.

Ben grabbed my shoulder. He studied the site for a moment.

"See the defenses?" he asked me. I didn't, but he pointed at what I'd thought were trashcans. "There. Motion sensitive."

"Oh." I was glad I hadn't just walked on in. "But..."

"Shhhh." Ben looked around, listening to something I couldn't hear.

On the other side of the crash site a gun cracked. Three guns fired back quickly. The pop of gunfire echoed through the trees where we hid for a half minute, then died off.

Someone screamed in frustration.

"Both sides are here," Ben said. "We're not the only ones that ran to the crash. But... you're all being too loud. You're disturbing Thanatos. No good will come of this."

I tried to get a better look around the crash site. I didn't want to walk in and get captured by mutineers.

Ben saw my movement. "Your friends are sheltering in that skip," he said confidently.

"How do you know that?" I asked.

"They don't have the same communications signatures as the other riggers I'm hearing around Thanatos." Ben turned around and tapped my shoulder with a terrifying missile launcher tube of a forearm. "Please look into that cheese for me, if you can, and keep hold of it. I have to go. I have to see about calming Thanatos. All this flying and fighting is waking things. I will find you again shortly."

I had no idea what he was talking about, but I nodded. I thought I recognized Lady Woodgrove's stiff posture in the distance, walking around the far edge of the crashed skip, though it was hard to tell from this distance in the shadows.

"If you need me again, just find that dismal swamp we met in. I'll be there, in the evenings. It's closer to the best bandwidth."

He slipped off into the forest, leaving me alone to pick my way through toward the skip.

"Lady Woodgrove?" I shouted, not daring to get any closer in case I was shot at.

Familiar faces peered around the edge of the skip. Dr. Armstrong, Lady Woodgrove, and Captain Garrik.

"Jane? Is that really you?" Lady Woodgrove asked, her voice penetrating the woods. "Mister Garrik, let her through!"

I stepped out and crossed the open area into camp. Once over some imaginary line, what I'd thought were trashcans powered up. A tiny whine filled the air again, and I noticed a faint line of blue create a border around the crash site.

Lady Woodgrove shook my hand formally, but with a crushing and excited grip. "Well done, Jane."

I gaped. Well done? That was it. *Please*. Not after everything I'd just done to keep the three of them alive.

Dr. Armstrong looked like he wanted to hug me, then decided it was inappropriate, so he tapped my shoulders like some awkward uncle.

A handful of Captain Garrik's riggers also milled about. I recognized one: Lincoln Merriweather. There was a fresh grave near the skip. I let my eyes slip past it. More death, I thought, a cloud of darkness settling in over me.

Maybe it would have been better for me to stay on Sargasso, bunkered down at the Inn. And even if I had died, it would have just been me. I could have saved lives by not dragging so many others into this.

These deaths were my fault. It felt like a heavy weight

pressing down on me. A tightness in my chest that made it hard to breathe sometimes.

"Jane Hawkins," Captain Garrik said, with a small smile. My mood lifted slightly with that quirk of his lips.

"I was hoping you would have taken the *Dorado*," I said to him.

"Outgunned. Argyros left some very dangerous men behind. We were lucky to get away and into Thanatos," Garrik said. And he glanced at the mound of dirt at the edge of camp.

I tried to suppress my disappointment at the thought of being trapped on Thanatos, but a tiny surge of panic ran through me.

I fought it down by telling them about Ben the Weapon. Garrik zeroed in on one of the details. "Cheese?"

"Cheese. And a chance to get home," I said.

"He could be a useful ally," Garrik said, slowly. "But I don't know if we're going to be able to promise him a ride home. I can still, however, deliver on the cheese."

Dr. Armstrong sat down on a box of supplies and sighed. "They ran to our crash site and tried to attack. We just barely got Captain Garrik's defense system pulled into place before they showed."

"Don't get mopey about it," Lady Woodgrove said sharply. "We have supplies, weapons, and Jane. A contact in Thanatos. And the riggers out there are slapping slow patches on, one after the other. They're barely able to function."

That sounded odd. I was about to ask about it, when a familiar voice hailed us. "Hello, Captain!"

"Argyros," I hissed, and turned around.

One of the silvered robotic bodies stood near the edge of the crash site's defense line.

Argyros sounded as if he were just casually calling for us across a crowded room. Calm.

"Can I talk to you?" he shouted.

Behind the robotic self, the human part of him stood back near one of the trees, leaning against it with folded hands. The last piece of himself stood just off to the side like a bodyguard.

"I'm not interested in anything he has to say," said Lady Woodgrove.

But Captain Garrik ignored her and walked forward to the thin line in the air. A laser tripwire, or just a warning, I thought. What I'd thought were trashcans pivoted to follow his movement.

Garrik and Argyros stood on either side of the line, facing each other. The rest of Argyros meandered up to the line as well, bold and unworried about the situation. One of Argyros's metal bodies nodded at me. "Jane."

I strung a series of curses together, and the human part of Argyros chuckled.

"Captain," he said, wiping the quick smile from his face, letting it congeal into something more serious. "We're in something of a predicament together."

"One *you* created," Garrik growled.

"Granted," he said in a carefully neutral tone. Argyros graciously swept a hand around. "Mistakes *were* made. But I'm trying to find us all a path out of this mess with no more bloodshed."

Mistakes were made, I thought. How slick of him to use words like that. Not 'I made a mistake,' but 'mistakes were made.' As if somehow the mistakes created themselves, and Argyros was embarrassed about them.

Those were not the words to describe a man who calmly wiped the blood off of all his hands after murdering someone.

"More likely you don't want to lose any more of your crew to attacking us to try and get Jane."

"It's more than just that," Argyros said. "The *Sparkflint*'s old countermeasures are turning on. We need to get to the treasure, and fast, and get out. The longer we battle, the more dangerous it gets in here."

"Again, not something we did."

Argyros lowered his voice, bargaining. "Help us, and I promise you I will give you safe passage and a share of my share of the treasure."

Captain Garrik nodded, but I could see that his posture was stiff with rage. "Is that what you came here to offer? Because the way I see it, we have Jane. We are secure here. And you can barely maintain a Consensus, Argyros. Your men are doping themselves, unable to control their own neurological processes. Think they're going to be able to ride a spar without my guidance?"

Argyros's reply snapped through the air, loud enough for all to hear. Garrick's words had needled him, and Argyros was angry. "Delaying won't save you. I swear, sit around much longer and those of you that die will be the lucky ones."

He spun around, his two robotic selves flanking his human body as they walked back into the woods.

"He's lying," I said, seeing Dr. Armstrong fidget with read outs in the air in front of him. He was looking at images of the riggers covered in patches. I'd had a realization about why Argyros was utterly wrong about his threats.

"About what?"

"Thanatos being dangerous," I said. "Do you think Ben would have been living here for so long by himself if it was so dangerous?"

Argyros disappeared into the shadows of the woods.

For a moment, the air was quiet.

Then three riggers burst out of the tree line. Gunshots and silent thwacks filled the air as railguns and traditional guns fired. I scrabbled and dove for cover behind the supply containers out on the ground.

Captain Garrik's defense system filled the air with cracks. Not gunshots. Lightning shot out and danced through the air, stabbing at the riggers bounding across the wet grass.

The nearest rigger slumped to the ground, her body blackened with burns, a wisp of smoke trailing from her clothing.

The other two retreated quickly, dragging the body of their comrade with them.

"I'll take the first watch," Captain Garrik said, his voice hushed. "They'll be back, we'll need to be vigilant."

He handed me a small, silvery pistol. It warmed to the touch of my fingers and made a 'snick' sound as it loaded. In the air, information appeared to my enhanced eyes. How to load it. Sighting information. Potential targets. Outcomes. How many bullets were inside it. All laid out in transparent graphics laid over the world around me.

"Hopefully you won't have to use it," Garrik said.

Chapter Twenty-Four

After Dr. Armstrong scanned me over to make sure I was okay, he ordered me to get some sleep. There was no night on Thanatos, just more blueish light that waxed and waned as we passed by other moons in our long orbit of the gas giant.

The idea of sleep seemed ridiculous. Not when I was expecting the riggers to rush the crash site and drag me away.

But inside, with the crashed skip's cool shadows and a few blankets pulled up around me, my scratchy eyes began to droop further and further.

How long had I been up? I couldn't remember. So much had happened. It felt like just a few hours. And yet at the same time the party we'd had after coming in to orbit near Thanatos felt like it had been held an entire lifetime away.

I had no idea what the truth was as I fell into a troubled, restless sleep.

A few hours later I bolted awake, seized by a sudden idea. *I was the map!* I had an inventory of Thanatos buried deep inside me.

In the cool quiet of the skip I breathed deep and banished everything around me from my vision. I looked past the stores, cots, and the people around me as my new eyes sought out hidden data that only I could see.

The digital tattoos beneath my skin glowed and then ripped free. Bright lines whipped around me as I twisted my neck. I began to follow them, pulling images of Thanatos closer in to me in order to study them.

Three dimensional wireframe models of the world around me exploded open with a fingertip's touch. I could pull the entire thing apart and explore every inch.

The cabin was getting overly cold. I shivered a little and ignored it.

I was onto something. I knew it.

There was more than just treasure on Thanatos. There had to be all manner of useful things hiding around.

Like a one person robotic maintenance pod, buried deep on the other side of Thanatos like a tick into a dog's neck. I stared at the blinking shape for a while, and then stood up.

Argyros and the captain planned a battle.

For a battle, Argyros would need riggers by his side.

The *Dorado* would be barely crewed.

The captain had put us on watches. Mine was not for another eight hours.

They might not even need me in eight hours, I thought. Not if I could sneak back aboard the *Dorado*. I looked down at the gun the captain had given me.

A minute later I slipped out of the skip and onto the ground.

The defense units recognized me now, they'd been programmed to not shoot at me. My feet broke the virtual no-pass lines in the air as I ran out into the trees.

A path plotted itself for my eyes in the air. This wasn't a crazed run through swamps and broken landscapes. I walked along the open trails and roads of Thanatos, skirting around the rigger camp nearby.

I jumped slightly as a tiger roared, heart in my throat. Argyros had brought his pet here?

I ran along the trail faster, imagining it running through the trees at me. But I wasn't chased. And the further I got from the crash site, the more I relaxed.

Overhead, Thanatos curved and stretched. A dome of land far above my head. A few clouds hung in the very center of Thanatos, drifting about aimlessly.

I reached the far endcap of Thanatos after several hours of walking. A mile-high wall in front of me. Nowhere to go but up.

A glass elevator, one of many that headed up toward the transparent center of the endcap like spokes, waited for me. I took it up, wincing at the creaking of old machinery.

The feeling of weight slowly slipped away as I rose into the air, looking out over Thanatos.

Through a smaller set of airlocks, human-sized, I found the pod and climbed in.

"What am I doing?" I asked myself as I strapped in.

The pod answered me by powering up. Controls flitted into the air, hovering over my fingers. Images swam into focus off to the side, dust swirling through them.

Clamps disengaged, and another airlock opened. Air vented to outer space.

I stared out into the blackness, my skin prickled with sweat.

"Okay," I said to myself. "Here goes nothing."

With a faint burst of energy, I kicked the pod out into the blackness of space outside of Thanatos. It was like playing a videogame, I thought, flying out of the far side of Thanatos and turning back toward the massive rocky cylinder. And certainly easier than trying to control a spar.

Ten minutes later, the long, spear-like shape of the *Dorado* loomed in front of me, and I smiled.

"Gotcha."

Chapter Twenty-Five

The pod struck the *Dorado*'s airlock with a clang and hiss. My ears popped as air rushed out. I unclipped my restraints and flew out of the pod and into the loading bay with my gun drawn, but nothing but silence waited for me. The bay was lit on with emergency lighting, and no crew came flying in to confront me.

Dorado had become a ghost ship. Empty metal corridors minimally lit. Distant creaking noises trickled through bulkheads and echoed from wall to wall.

I floated around, nervously jack-rabbiting from handhold to handhold.

A gunshot startled me as it reverberated through the corridors.

I found Colorado Jones hanging in the cockpit. A rigger's body hung in the air several feet in front of Jones, slowly spinning toward a wall. Large bubbles of blood filled the air, wobbling along with the body. I stared at it, forgetting to raise my own gun.

"Stay right there!" Jones shouted at me. His glazed eyes flicked slowly from me to the body. "Are you Jane, or some kind of trick? You shouldn't be here."

"I'm Jane," I said, and looked away from the dead rigger to Jones.

"Okay. Good." There were dosage patches along his forearm, and Jones looked just about ready to pass out. His hands shook as he pulled out a med packet and ripped it open.

He sighed as he slapped the drugs against the side of his neck. That gave me the time I needed to pull my gun out and point it at him.

"Throw your gun aside," I ordered.

Jones growled, but did so. The gun twirled end over end and clattered against a chair. It rebounded, but then tangled in the straps well out of his reach. "What do you think you're doing, Hawkins?"

"I'm your captain, now, Mr. Jones," I said. I reached down inside and found calm. I was in control. I had a plan. I knew how to turn this all around.

"Really?" Jones sounded dubious, and maybe a little amused as well.

Normally that would set me off. Hackled and angry. But instead I just smiled at him. Unperturbed.

Where had this newfound sense of self come from? I felt like I'd accessed a higher plane of functioning. Certainty oozed from my pores with a heat that made my fingers crackle as they grabbed the side of the bulkhead.

"Everyone down there is going to end up killing each other if we don't do something to stop them," I said.

"And how, Miss Hawkins, do you plan on doing that?" Jones asked.

I looked at him cooly. He looked back at me through a chemical fog, thinking about my words.

"First, I'm taking control of the *Dorado*. Once Argyros realizes he has lost control of this ship, he'll realize he has nothing left to bargain with," I explained.

"Argyros will storm the ship. You might not live through that," Jones growled. "Map inside you or not, Argyros won't allow someone taking his ship."

"We're going to dock the *Dorado* to Thanatos so my people get aboard before his. Then we move back. Forget the treasure, we'll have the ship."

"*You* can't move this ship," Jones laughed. "You're more likely to rip it apart than move it."

I narrowed my eyes.

"The hell I can't," I said through gritted teeth.

I created a Consensus, right there in the room. But it was different than the one I'd trained in and felt throughout the ship when Captain Garrik had been flinging the *Dorado* through space. The digital air was dark, the neural static fuzzy with strong presence all around.

Jones closed his eyes and swore.

"You have the black spot within you, don't you?"

I thought back to the swirling darkness on Villem's palm when he'd been jerked around like a marionette back in the Inn, so long ago.

"Black spot?"

"The *Sparkflint*'s old Consensus," Jones said with a croak. "We had to be able to trust that everyone would follow all orders under Consensus, so it could take over all limbic functions. Control your mind, your body, everything. Just like your hand is a part of your body, when you were in the *Sparkflint*'s Consensus, you were a part of the whole. It's dripping from your pores."

Jones sounded genuinely scared.

"Villem Osteonidus gave it to me, with the map, and upgrades," I said.

Jones reached up to his neck and slowly peeled off his patch. Then he yanked the ones on his forearms off.

"I won't fight it. I'll help you get the *Dorado* docked to Thanatos."

I could feel his consciousness swirling up to join the bleak maelstrom I'd created in the air as his neural implants sped up, freed of the drugs.

"You should get rid of the body," I told him, looking at the large blobs of blood wobbling through the air. "Through the nearest airlock."

"I…" he looked at the body. "I can still hear echoes of his mind in the air. He wouldn't like that."

"He's dead," I said coldly, gripped by that commanding posture I'd taken since boarding the ship. Another death on my hands, and suddenly I just wanted to move forward with my plan as quickly as possible. Nothing else was as important as stopping more death. "It doesn't matter."

Colorado Jones looked at me, a haunted expression settling into his face. He kicked forward through the air, grabbed the body, and threw it out of the cockpit.

"Then it doesn't matter whether he rattles around our

corridors until we dock with Thanatos and we can take care of him properly, does it?"

"Fair enough," I muttered.

"I'm going to go find a spar to ride," he said.

"You'll do it from here. Where I can see you," I told him.

"That adds lag to the control."

"I know," I said. My voice was strong and unbendable, and carried out into the virtual as well as the audible. Jones shivered. "But do it anyway."

PREPARE FOR ACCELERATION the ship's systems said, sending my voice all throughout the empty corridors and bays throughout.

"Aye, Captain of the Consensus," Jones muttered. "Make sure to strap in, Miss. We'll be barely able to control her."

A loud creaking sound accompanied a shiver along the *Dorado*'s hull. A single spar, controlled by Jones, dipped ever so slightly into the invisible wind.

The ship wobbled, and Jones grunted. We flailed across the space between us and Thanatos.

The spar Jones controlled ripped free of the *Dorado*. Alarms wailed, sections of the ship shut themselves down to prevent air loss.

"Mr. Jones?"

We were barely moving, he'd just nudged the ship along. But without a deployed spar to slow us back down, we were gently careening toward the open doors of Thanatos.

"Mr. Jones!"

Was he doing this on purpose? I saw the sweat all over his forehead as he concentrated, some of it mixed with the blood floating around the air. He seemed to be trying as hard as he could.

I grabbed the virtual controls of the nearest spar I could get online and deployed it. Just dipped it into the invisible maelstrom as Jones shouted at me.

For a picosecond, I was triumphant. I dipped into the winds outside and slowed the ship down. Hull plates bucked and tore, whipped by sudden stress on the single spar's contact point.

And then the spar tore away, leaving a massive gash in the hull.

More structural complaints peppered my vision from the ship's systems.

And no time to try again, because now the nose of the *Dorado* eased in through the airlock gates. The ship struck metal and rock. Jones screamed, but then I realized it was the sound of scraping, not screaming. Metal on metal. Metal on rock. Crunching.

The Consensus exploded in warnings, alarms, reports. Data flung itself aggressively at me, trying to get my attention. Numbers, graphics, and exploded blueprints whirled like a hurricane around me. Unsteady cameras from points all throughout the ship presented their live images to me, trying to give me eyes on the damage.

I saw rooms buckle, ghostly wisps of air fleeing through cracks in the hull.

Now I was the one screaming, shutting my eyes and trying to get it all to stop hammering at the insides of my brain to the point where a tiny trickle of blood began to leak out of my nostril.

And then, with a final, sickening crunch that stabbed me with the certainty that I had now made things far worse than better, the *Dorado* lurched to a lumbering stop.

Chapter Twenty-Six

I spun head over heels and struck the opposite wall. Gasping for breath I struggled to orient myself in the rain of debris that clattered down through the air.

"Don't move," Colorado Jones said.

Blood leaked into the air from a gash on his left leg, seeping out into the air. He aimed his gun at me, unwavering and calm.

The body of the man he'd killed floated past the cockpit doors, arms stretched wide, teeth white in the blue light.

"You're infected," Jones jerked his head at the body just as it glided off further down the ship. "Just like he was."

"Don't be ridiculous," I reassured him, my voice calming and smooth.

"*Sparkflint's* got you." He ripped open foil packets with his free, trembling hand and teeth, then slapped them against his neck. One after the other as he spoke.

"No one *has* me," I said, angry. I stared at the barrel of the gun pointed at me, waiting for it to dip or twitch.

But Jones held it steady enough, tracking me as I very slowly moved through the cockpit's air, pushed along by air currents.

"I served aboard the *Sparkflint*," he said. "I can feel the danger in you. There will be blood on your hands soon. You know how we got so that it took a fleet to hunt us down and kill the ship?"

I shook my head. If I could keep him talking, then he wouldn't be shooting. "How?"

"The *Sparkflint* didn't have a human captain, like your Captain Garrik, coordinating the Consensus. The *Sparkflint* was the coordinator of the Consensus, and it was created by each of the crew giving a piece of our minds over to the ship. A monstrous sort of patchwork artificial intelligence that represented us all."

"I know some of the stories," I said, thinking back to the books I enjoyed as a child.

Jones studied my face intently. "You know nothing. We had to do it, in order to survive the creatures we fought. Because the *Sparkflint* was the ship embodied, it could make decisions that a captain couldn't. It made us more dangerous, more willing to push the limit of neural endurance, and sparflight. It was the edge we needed to stop the aliens from wiping us out. We had to hand over our humanity to save humanity. The soldier's choice. Only… when the war was over, no one considered us soldiers anymore. And the hunts continued."

Now the man smiled.

I didn't smile back.

"We forged one Consensus to rule us all, and in the darkness of space, bind us." Jones laughed as I looked at him blankly. "You're not a fan of classical literature, I take it?"

"You let yourselves become something less than human," I said. "You were too weak to break yourselves free."

Jones curled his lips.

"Too weak?" He slapped a last patch on his neck. "I've been fighting the *Sparkflint* since we arrived here, ignoring its whisper, deep in the back of my head. Keeping myself drugged enough that it can't access my higher neural processors. The ghost of that ship somehow ended up here on Thanatos. You, on the other hand, my girl, are a fully acting agent of the *Sparkflint's* Consensus programming. I can smell it."

Fear and disgust bloomed in me. I shook my head. "You're talking a lot of nonsense."

"And the only way to stop you," Jones continued. "Is the same way I stopped him."

He pointed toward the cockpit's doors. The crewman he'd killed had rebounded off a bulkhead somewhere and was drifting back the other way, passing by us again.

He was down slow, drugged by the patches. Sweating and nervous. Tired. Edgy. Strung out.

I was soaked in sweat, the tattoos under my skin blazing in the digital realm and filling his eyes with their brilliance.

He jumped at me.

Sped up, it seemed like he moved in slow motion. I saw the muscles in his shoulder twitch. They transferred energy down his arm. A bicep rippled. The forearm rippled. The gun's barrel slowly inched toward me.

Jones tightened his forefinger slightly on the trigger. It moved down, pressed against flesh as it was forced closer to that inevitable moment where it would click.

His eyes blinked ever so slowly. His jaw clenched, determination in his expression.

I'd seen that look before. Argyros's human face, right before he'd leapt to kill Red Ruth.

My hand was up, the pistol aimed, and I fired two shots before I could even register the physical reaction. Jones shot once.

My shots flipped me end-over-end backwards, the reaction to shooting. But something else had also struck my shoulder, adding to the spin.

Blood filled my field of vision.

And then the pain exploded in my shoulder. A supernova of compressed stabbing that radiated from the corner of my upper arm.

I squeezed tears out of the corners of my eyes as I struck a wall. Dizzied for a moment, I lost my bearings.

As everything swam back into focus, I stared at the body of Colorado Jones on the other side of the cockpit.

He stared off into space, unseeing. A bullet hole in the center of his forehead.

Chapter Twenty-Seven

I shivered and threw the pistol aside in sudden disgust and stared at my hands. What had I just done?

The movement burned, my right shoulder stabbing me so hard my heart skipped a beat and I gasped. But that helped me realize that Jones had meant to kill me.

I hadn't killed him. I wasn't Argyros. I'd killed in order to save my own life.

Jones was the killer. Not me.

And I might still die, I realized, yanking the corner of my shirt back to look at my shoulder. Just past the edge of my bra strap, on the tip of my shoulder, was a ragged chunk of bleeding flesh where the bullet had passed through skin and muscle.

It was bleeding badly, but it was just a glancing shot.

I pulled up a query to the ship's systems, and a line appeared in the virtual air that led me to a first aid kit bolted on a corridor wall.

The ship felt claustrophobic and oppressive. The air still and choked with death. I'd done what needed done. I didn't need to stay here, I needed to let everyone know the ship was here.

Sweating and feverish, I fumbled my way out of the *Dorado*. The great gates of the endcap airlock had closed behind her after the horrible crash. The forward doors were open to the interior of Thanatos, so I didn't need to use the pod to escape. I could just make my way out and use one of the elevators to get down to the distant, curved ground of the interior.

It was getting hard to breathe, and my vision blurred a bit as I stumbled through trees trying to make my way back to the distant crash site.

This fever had to be coming from the wound on my

shoulder. An infection, I thought.

I paused, disoriented and panting. Wasn't I close to the site?

Something orange crashed through the bushes on my right. I whirled, and realized I had nothing to protect myself with. I'd left the gun back in the cockpit.

Argyros's tiger leapt out from behind a tree and pinned me to the ground, the massive paw a boulder on my chest that shoved me hard into the soft ground.

The face, large enough I'd would have barely been able to wrap my hands around it, peered closely at me. Whiskers tickled me. The tiger huffed, moistening my face with the rancid smell of decay.

PIECE OF MEAT! it declared enthusiastically in the virtual space around us. Anyone with neural upgrades anywhere nearby could hear it. PIECE OF MEAT!

I wasn't sure whether the tiger thought I was a piece of meat, or whether it was asking me for some. Like a trapped mouse, I just froze, hyper-aware of the clawed paw holding me in place.

"Well," said a familiar voice. One of Argyros's robotic pieces, the once-polished chassis now spattered with mud and leaves, crouched down beside me.

The tiger removed its paw. I took a deep breath of air and scuttled back away from it. I slammed the back of my head into Argyros's other metallic body.

His human third stepped out from the bush. "Miss Hawkins, delighted to see you again," he said.

I stood up and clenched my jaw, looked straight at him and the other riggers standing in the shadows behind him.

"I'm not scared of any of you," I shouted. And then I sneered. "Particularly not you, Jonathan Argyros. I remember your first day diving into the bloody mess of combat; your horror, the stench of fear in the Consensus. *I see you...*"

Argyros blanched for a split second, then leapt at me with that same animalistic speed he'd leapt at Red Ruth. I screamed and punched at his face, but two steel-hard metallic arms pinned from the side.

He slapped my neck.

I didn't understand for a second. Then a warm, treacly feeling slid through me. A weight evaporated from my head. A cool patch clung to the side of my neck, delivering heavy tranquilizers.

Argyros added four more, until I looked like Colorado Jones had.

"It's a good thing you showed up," he said conversationally as I tried to open my mouth and drooled slightly out of the corner of my lips. "Only six of us riggers left here, after fighting with your captain. And I'm losing them. They're fighting the old Blackspot Consensus. It's what hangs over the air everywhere in here. The ghosts of the old crew, people long since passed, left in computers and networks still running inside this old tomb. But with you back, we'll have direction again. And I can channel that."

As I lolled about, coming down out of a neural high, I could feel the heat radiating from the back of my head. I'd been overheated. The sweat almost sizzled on my skin.

Argyros dragged me across the glade, past several cots protected by slabs of see-through plastic lean-tos. He picked me up, passed me from a set of hands another set of his hands, and dumped me into a container filled with ice cubes and water.

Cold stabbed me. I thrashed and screamed at the sudden chill.

Argyros held me down in the water, his human face staring at me.

"What you just told me back there," he said calmly, "was something only the *Sparkflint* could have remembered. So, as useful as you are, right now, I need you to get control of yourself. The crew won't say it out loud, but in the Consensus, they're begging me to kill you and head back to the ship. All they can think about is running for safety. But then, they were always weak minds."

Argyros slapped a patch on his forearm and sighed.

I bobbed in the freezing water and stared up at the lands far overhead, obscured by an occasional cloud. I'd been tricked. I'd run away from the safety of the camp without telling anyone because I'd woken up with the idea of looking for a pod. And then I'd run off to use it.

And I had dragged the *Dorado* back into Thanatos.

Why?

I'd thought it was because *I* wanted to end the fighting. But now, looking at the scared me and thinking about Colorado Jones, I shivered. Not due to the ice water, but with fear.

Something had been whispering to me. Something buried so deep into my own mind, I had thought it was me.

I remembered Villem's tendons bulging as he fought against the invisible strings dragging him out that night back in the Inn.

"I've risked a lot for fortune," Argyros said. He leaned forward. "I'll risk even more for *this* fortune. I'll gladly risk their lives. But not ours. Do you understand?"

I nodded. He had drawn a circle around the two of us. For now, at least.

A triumphant grin licked the corners of Argyros's human eyes. He had what he wanted now. The map. Me.

"Look," one of the riggers shouted.

She pointed at the *Dorado*. We all looked up to the ship-sized airlock at the center of the endcap. Things moved about in the gloomy blue light and shadows. Machines were marching into the *Dorado*'s holds.

Thick, metal tentacles reached out from the walls and grasped the ship's hull. Sparks flew. More machines poured out of invisible nooks, swarming the ship like shiny ants.

I stood up in the container of freezing water, waves lapping at my calves. "What's happening?"

Argyros deflated. His human face paled with shock, and his jaw trembled slightly. That hungry fire I had come to recognize faded from his eyes, snuffed out by the scene in the distance.

Two of the riggers jerked forward, as if being pulled

toward the ship. They swore and stumbled to the ground, regaining control of themselves.

I saw the black spots appear on their hands. Swirling, malicious, and frenetic with energy.

Back in the distance the *Dorado* continued to be transformed by Thanatos. And then, under my feet, I felt rumbling. Machines rushing through corridors far below our feet to get to the ship.

"What's happening?" I asked again.

Argyros looked at me. "Come with me," he growled. "I'm going to need your map. Now."

He yanked me out of the cold bath.

"Damn you, get up. We have to get moving. Get up!" He turned on one of the riggers lying on the ground and kicked him.

He moved around, shaking everyone into action to gain a semblance of control of his crew. I watched him hand out dosage patches.

"How many of those do you have left?" I asked, watching riggers tear them open.

"Enough," Argyros hissed at me. "Now, it's time we set out for that treasure."

He said that in a snarl of sorts. But it wasn't the snarl of a composed leader. Argyros was scared, and hiding it with action.

He looked like he had seen a ghost.

Chapter Twenty-Eight

I led the riggers through the stinking forests and failed swamps of Thanatos. My hands shook with exhaustion. Burned out, I could barely blink without half falling asleep on my feet.

The riggers spoke in half-whispers, and with their real voices. They were like nervous, shiny rats trying to avoid drawing attention to themselves.

I followed the threads of blue and red lines, hunting treasure. Or fleeing something.

"Villem was a master at reprogramming systems," Argyros said. "He built what's in you off a seed he scraped from the *Sparkflint*. He thought, if he used the *Flint*'s core code, he could use it to let himself take control of the Blackspot Consensus. Slip through the *Sparkflint*'s world. It was his life's work. And in the end, he hid away from us rather than hand it over. He infected you with it. This would have all been quick and easy had he just handed the damn thing over to us."

The bushes off to our sides rustled.

We all slowed, the riggers holding up their weapons and forming a rough circle.

"Who's there?"

"Fetch the aft weapons!" cried a deep voice.

"Aww, shit," one of the riggers swore.

I let my visions of schematics and maps fade away.

"Ben's dead," Argyros said, eyes narrowing. "And I can hear whoever is saying that rustle about over there. Show yourself!"

I sat down in the dirt, too exhausted to continue. There was a vision seeping up from the bottom of my mind. I could see the movement of supplies to the *Dorado* almost as if I were the one directing their movements.

Villem had hacked me deep into being able to see a lot

about Thanatos, not just maps.

Weapons. The *Dorado* was being armored with pulse weapons, artillery, extra neural networks, and stronger deck plating.

It was being turned into a warship, right before our eyes.

"Show yourself!" Argyros screamed again.

Ben stepped out into the midst of our group. One of the riggers screamed and shot at him. Ben shrugged the attack off and struck back with a giant barrel.

The rigger slumped to the ground, blood running from a nasty cut to his head.

"I am Ben. Remember me Argyros?"

Argyros stared.

"Fetch the aft weapons," Ben said quietly. "That is what you said to me, before you all tried to kill me. I remember it quite clearly to this day."

Argyros put a hand to his hip. "I remember who you used to be," he said. "But you can't be alive."

"Any more than the *Sparkflint* could be alive? Any more than *you* could be alive?"

Both men, more machine than man, stared at each other for a long moment.

"I want to talk to Jane," Ben said, finally.

"Why?" Argyros asked suspiciously.

"There's no treasure for you here," Ben said. "Come, Jane, lead them to the top of the hill. I will show them."

The motley group straggled up after me. There was a crater at the tip of the hill. A digging device had carved the sides of it clean, and raw dirt had been exposed to the elements of Thanatos for a long while. Enough to have formed a solid crust.

"It should be here," I said, blinking. My virtual eyes showed a wealth of rare metals and gems, high quality diamonds capable of handling superconducting computing.

But there was really nothing but gray earth here.

"The ghosts of the *Sparkflint* haunt Thanatos," Ben said in a tired voice. "And you came back and woke them. Woke *it*.

The *Sparkflint*. This isn't just the trove, this is a tomb. Do you all understand? And when you struck that ship against the tomb, you woke everything. The point defense system came online, and everything else awoke."

"It can't be alive," Argyros said. "I saw the ship die. Ripped apart by fire."

"The *Sparkflint* was a machine. A digital consciousness, man," Ben said. "It had itself backed up. Synchronized itself whenever the ship came here to its trove. That was the real treasure."

Argyros looked sick.

Ben pointed an empty barreled forearm in the direction of the *Dorado*'s hull. "It's had decades to mull over its defeat and plan its revenge on the world that destroyed it and left it hiding here."

The walls of Thanatos shivered, and the clanking echoes coming from the miles-away, ship-sized airlock ceased. The tiny random glints of far-off robotic welders ceased.

Two spars flicked open like switchblades and the air around them *bent* and rippled as they engaged with the unseen energy flowing around them.

Invisible vortices whipped free and dented the walls around the ship. Energy crackled and spat, warping the air all throughout Thanatos with earth-shaking thunder.

Hoses and clamps burst free from the hull as the ship backed away. As it did so, the massive airlock doors rumbled slowly shut in front of it. A dark and heavy storm that had swirled somewhere deep in the back of my mind drifted away with the ship.

I felt like I could stand up inside my own head.

"Once again, marooned," Ben whimpered as we all stared at the implacable wall in the distance.

Chapter Twenty-Nine

Argyros very casually tapped my forearm and handed me a pistol. One of his metallic selves blocked him from view of the other riggers as he whispered into my ear, "The Sparkflint was never one for leaving loose ends."

I almost dropped the weapon, thinking about the feel of the last pistol I'd held kicking back in my hand as I fired at Colorado Jones.

"You got us in this mess," one of the riggers said, turning on Argyros. Fiber optic cables hung from the back his neck, dangling down past his shoulders.

Argyros spread out his selves. "Now, Jorge, you know we all wanted to get the Sparkflint's treasures."

"You're the one who kept in contact, who tracked us down. You arranged all this," said another rigger, stepping forward. "You called yourself the captain of the Consensus, didn't you?"

A pained grin flicked across Argyros's lips. "Yes. Yes I did."

"CEO of our little venture, right?"

Some sort of weapon slithered down around Jorge's right arm. A barrel appeared near his wrist.

"Let's not..." Argyros began.

Jorge raised his hand to fire, but Argyros gunned him down first. The rigger grunted in surprise, huddling forward as blood gushed out from between the hands he clapped to his chest.

"Jane, get down," Argyros snapped at me as the other riggers dove for cover behind bushes and trees. I stared as gunfire ripped through the wilting vegetation at them.

Relief washed over me as Lady Woodgrove stalked toward me. "Damnit, Jane, get down!" she shouted.

The imperious sound of her voice startled me into

motion, and I got down on the dirt as Doctor Armstrong and Captain Garrik stomped through the bushes.

I lay on my side, looking over at Jorge as he stopped groaning to himself. Eventually he closed his eyes in pain and just... stopped.

Just past his neck, I saw the thick boots of two riggers throw dirt into the air as they ran. Woodgrove calmly followed in their tracks, shooting after them.

Bullets struck trees, spitting splinters into the air. Leaves tore and fluttered slowly down through the blue air toward the ground.

And then a heavy silence settled to the ground.

"Are you okay, Jane?" Doctor Armstrong asked, squatting next to me.

"I'm okay," I said, and both of us pretended not to hear the quaver in my voice. He helped me to my feet.

Woodgrove stared off into the trees with murder in her eyes, her lips curled. Captain Garrik had ripped a sleeve off his shirt to look at a nasty cut on his bicep, but seemed okay. He met my glance with a quick, curt nod that only self-assured authority could give.

I almost burst out laughing.

We were all dead people, fighting like it mattered.

None of it mattered anymore. Who was on what side? Who was rich, or poor. Captain or mutineer.

Argyros had thrown his weapons to the ground and surrendered. His human part staggered over to a furry orange form in the shadows. The two robotic bodies moved in from either side, one cradling the animal's head, the other crouching nearby in a defeated posture.

With shoulders slumped, Argyros's kneeled in front of the body of the tiger and ran his hands over the massive cat's front paw.

"What do we do about him?" Dr. Armstrong asked.

Captain Garrik glanced over. "He surrendered."

"He *caused* this mess," Woodgrove snapped. "We chain him up."

"And do what?" Ben rumbled, something inside of him hissing as he started to walk over toward Argyros. "Take him to jail where? What court will he stand in? Do you see any things like this here?"

He brushed past Woodgrove, who still had her weapons raised, as if to turn them on Argyros. She didn't try to stop the strange assortment of man and metallic parts as he walked over to Argyros.

With a great sigh he knelt next to Argyros's human form and put a hand on his shoulder.

And said nothing.

After a long moment, Argyros's shoulders quivered slightly. All three bodies, in synch. Then he cleared his throats and stood up again.

"Comfort?" he asked Ben. "Why?"

"I could hold a grudge against you for eternity. Make you pay. But I spent decades alone in this tomb. I wouldn't wish that fate on my worst enemy. And now it is your fate as well. You've lost everything, Argyros, and now you're marooned forever with me. And you unleashed a hell that will attack our homeworld and everything on it we love. You need all the comfort you can get, Argyros."

Argyros's ashy face looked at each of us. In a flash, I realized Ben was getting his revenge, and we were watching it happen. Argyros could barely walk toward us. The loss of his pet self had been a final straw, something that reached deep into his broken self and yanked.

Ben wasn't done. He looked back at the tiger's body, artificial eyes and cameras snicking and refocusing.

"Poor thing. It had only you."

Argyros pointedly did not turn around. Or say anything.

A memory bubbled its way up through the back of my brain. Something Ben had said when we first met.

I watched the two men as I tried to dig through my mind.

Ben's creaky voice continued. "Imagine all those poor souls, those innocent children, looking up at the stars right now. How can they even imagine what's about to come down out of the dark for them? All because of your greed. What is my comfort? Nothing in the big picture. You will need all you can get, to live with yourself. If you can, my old friend."

Argyros slowly rubbed his temple, and then stood up straight with a hint of defiance. He said nothing, but it was clear the moment of Ben's ability to hurt him had passed.

"I guess we'll both stand in this hell we've created together, *old friend*," Argyros said.

"But that's not true, is it Ben?" I blurted out.

The cobbled-together cyborg cocked his head. "What's not true?"

Ben stepped forward, and I was suddenly reminded of how large he was. Those machined pistons under his biceps, they held those massive weaponized forearms up. And they could crush me like a little bug for revealing a secret of his.

I should have whispered this to the Captain. Or Woodgrove. Seen what they thought about it.

But then, whispers and plots had done so much for us, hadn't they?

I stepped forward.

"What you just said, it's not true. I remember what you told me that first time we met, Ben."

The mild accusation hung in the air as Ben just stood silently.

"Ben? Do you remember?"

"And what did I say, the first time we met?" Ben asked in a low voice.

"You said you were planning to leave, that you had a way off Thanatos," I said.

"I did, did I?" Ben mumbled. "Perceptive little thing, you are. Very full of memory and other neat tricks."

I folded my arms. *Little thing?* But I bit my lip. Maybe I was, next to him. I waited. And we all stared at Ben fidgeting as he stood in place.

"It's not a good idea," Ben said, finally. He looked at Argyros. "It could go very wrong. It's a last resort. Better than suicide… maybe."

"Tell us," I begged. A tiny piece of hope bloomed in me as I imagined some small ship, grafted onto a spare spar. Or a device that used all of Thanatos's energy to transmit an emergency signal.

"I was going to transmit myself home," Ben said.

"Transmit?" I asked, not sure what to make of that work.

But Doctor Armstrong looked thoughtful. "Like the mouse?"

Ben creaked and turned to look at the doctor. "Like the mouse."

"What?" I had no idea what they were all talking about.

"You can use quantum bits to transmit things, with programmable matter on the other side," Doctor Armstrong said. "Some ultra-rich used to, back when the attacks on ships got to be too much, transmit extremely valuable artifacts. The original would be scanned, down to the atom, destroyed in the process. And recreated, to the atom, on the other side."

"And they did it to a mouse?" I asked, and looked over at Ben.

Argyros was suddenly interested. "The bits needed to do it would be a fortune."

"It bankrupted the company that did it. A mouse's weight of bits? That's an obscene waste of wealth," Lady Woodgrove said.

"And besides, we don't have the *Sparkflint*'s treasure, do we?" Argyros said pointedly. He was staring closely at Ben, head cocked slightly. "No diamonds. No pieces of gold. No bits. Right, Ben?"

The giant cyborg stirred. "Well," it said in a gravelly voice. "That's not true. We do have all the treasure. I moved it."

Chapter Thirty

B etween the rocky outer skin of Thanatos, but under the wetlands and grasses and air of the interior access tunnels that crisscrossed through rock and machinery, a set of tunnels overlapped in a maze that did not appear on any of the maps I had been infected with.

"You've been busy down here," Argyros said to Ben.

"I hid," Ben said. "From the ghosts."

The cavern he led us to was a dark, dimly lit space carved crudely out of the rock. The top arched a good thirty feet over our head, and our footsteps echoed as we walked.

But despite the dim light, the walls of the cavern glinted and twinkled as mounds of treasure reflected light. Pulled free of their containers, jewels and gold bullion had been scooped up by machines and dumped onto the rock floors like mere gravel piles.

We all stopped. I knew that it was all useless to us. We couldn't eat it, and it couldn't save us from being marooned, but I still shivered with greed.

I was stepping on coins. Real gold coins. Yes, it was just a metal. Nothing more than a metal. A metal that humans had imbued with legendary impact. It was just a symbol, a promise of barter, or labor. Ben would have given up most of it for some *cheese*.

And yet…

There were diamonds covered in dust and crushed into the soft soil of the ground. Everyone was transfixed. I looked around at Woodgrove and Armstrong, who licked their lips. Even Captain Garrik's eyes were wide.

Argyros just grinned knowingly, and winked at me.

"Where's the dragon that guards all this?" I joked, trying to break the reverent tension.

"It flew away," Ben said.

Right.

He led us in between the glittering piles, through six foot high stacks of gold bricks that we all brushed with our fingertips as we passed.

A machine stood in a hollow. It lit up as we approached, screens flickering on and power humming through it. Hypercoolant cables, thick like metal boa snakes, ran away from it to hide underneath piles of treasure and snaked off to leech power from the innards of Thanatos.

Large radiator fans spread outwards, and the air around them rippled. I felt the heat in the room build.

The machine was hard to make out. It looked like Ben himself: pieces of hardware all bolted together to create something they were never meant to do. Machines lay scattered around the room, connected together. Maybe even pieces of Thanatos helped run it, via the fat cables.

"My life's work," Ben said, walking unsteadily around the core of the machine; a capsule cracked in half. Like a porcupine, thousands of needles spiked the shell of the capsule, with wires trailing from each.

Lady Woodgrove walked over to the edge of the machine. She leaned close to the thick base of the needles, then followed the wires back to fist-sized black boxes at their ends.

"Damn," she said in a soft voice.

It took a lot to awe the Lady Woodgrove, and this machine had done just that.

Each box had a code etched into its side. In the virtual it unpacked and presented a manifest: quantum entangled bits. Ready to be used.

And somewhere far away on Earth, as each of these bits was used here, the other entangled half would be affected.

"There's a problem," Lady Woodgrove said, no longer enthralled by the black boxes that were worth more to her than all the gold in the entire cavern. She tapped her fingers in the air, swiping screens that were visible only to her aided eyes. "There are not enough bits."

"It will be close," Ben said. "I will have to leave many

pieces of myself behind."

"It won't be close," Woodgrove said firmly. "There's too much mass."

"What about you?" Doctor Armstrong asked.

"Same problem."

"Damn it," Armstrong swore. His jaw trembled slightly. I realized that he was scared.

Here we were, standing in the middle of a trove of treasure beyond almost imagination, none of us even gave it a second glance now. We all stared at the machine.

I swallowed. Less mass. Smaller person.

No one was looking at me on purpose. Even Argyros's heads all looked pointedly at the machine and not me.

But it was obvious, wasn't it?

"Will it work on me?" I asked, softly.

Armstrong waved a hand at me. Hidden instruments mapped my form and sucked it into a virtual space for her to examine. Her fingers flicked this way and that, and then she nodded.

"Probably."

The heavy word thudded to the ground between us like a bar of gold.

"Probably?" Armstrong asked. "Just probably? How probably? She's too young. We can't risk her life on this with probably. She's just a girl, we…"

I raised a slightly trembling finger. *Just a girl?* My finger steadied and I glared.

"Hey!"

The sharp shout shut him up.

Everyone looked at me now. "*Probably* is about as good as any one of us ever gets. Probably is better than a lifetime marooned here, slowly dying. Losing our minds."

I glanced involuntarily at Ben who shuffled his feet.

"We don't really know if this will work," Armstrong protested. "And we don't know if we have enough quantum material to send you. That's two big 'ifs.' At the very least, we should wait to do more tests with the machine."

"The *Sparkflint* is on its way back to Earth for revenge," I
said. "After being trapped here. Do you think we have time?
Because we don't. We can be marooned, or we can send me
back now. Those are our two choices. *That's it.* Just because I'm
young doesn't mean I don't understand the crap situation we're
in."

My heart beat so fast, the adrenaline came so thick, I
could feel it all in the back of my throat.

I moved before anyone could stop me, stepping over
cables and boxes and jumping into the cocoon-shaped pod at
the center. "This is *my* choice," I shouted over everyone's
objections.

"Let her go," Argyros said.

Everyone turned on him. He must have known that
would happen, but he didn't look even the slightest bit
bothered by the blazing, surface-of-the-sun hot anger aimed his
way.

"You, of all people?" Woodgrove asked from between
clenched teeth.

"Me, of all people," Argyros replied. "When did you gain
the moral high ground, my dear Lady Woodgrove? When you
put Jane aboard a ship full of riggers you didn't know? When
you exposed her to the wilds and dangers of traveling between
the depths of interstellar space? Ships get hit by debris. Go
missing. People die out here. But for your own gain, you put
her life at risk. So *don't* lecture me. Each of us helped push her
to this point."

One of his metal selves bowed deeply, ironically, to Lady
Woodgrove.

She muttered something I couldn't quite pick up.

"Oh, but let us not forget," Argyros said, raising an
eyebrow. "That if we look back far enough, that she is the one
that got the map of Villem. Got infected by the *Sparkflint*'s core
data. And getting that back to Earth, that can help them design
something to fight it. Yes, none of us would be here, Jane, if it
weren't for you. Isn't that right?"

I looked him right in the eye. "You're right, Argyros. So

send me back," I said.

I pulled on the edge of the pod's lid.

Inside the sarcophagus-like space, with nothing but circuitry and probes staring me right in the eye, I tried not to panic. Apparently I was a little claustrophobic.

"Ben, send me back," I shouted.

"But Miss Jane…" his voice murmured at me from around the suffocating darkness.

"Ben, send me back to Earth and I swear I'll come back for you with a ship packed from spar to spar with nothing but cheese. You name the cheese, I'll be bringing it back. I'm talking sampler packs, blocks, wheels, cubes, you name it. I'll tow you a moon-sized wedge of whatever your favorite is. Please."

The silence pushed in at me for a moment, adding weight to the darkness. My breathing sounded flat and muted.

"Ben?" I called out.

"Now there's an image to lift a marooned soul," he finally said, with what sounded like a crack in his voice. Almost as if he'd teared up a little.

"Then let's do it." My own voice cracked too. But not because I was thinking about cheese.

"Okay," Ben said. "This is going to sting… all over. So brace for it."

"Sting?" I asked, voice rising.

"Well, each atom that's read by the machine destroys it as it is being transmitted," Ben muttered.

"Wait, what?" I tried to push the pod open to argue, raising my right hand and pushing. More angry words were just waiting. Ready to go.

And then a warm fire spread through me.

It was followed by the feeling of being ripped apart into trillions of different pieces as my eyes widened.

Chapter Thirty-One

I'm not one to scream.
In fact I found it generally rather demeaning. A loss of control. Not my style. Uncool.

But the sensation of being flipped inside out and back again after being set on digital fire got way inside my head. The idea that I'd been ripped apart, transmitted light years across space, and then...

I was screaming.

I'd started screaming in the pod, but I wasn't in the pod anymore. I was standing inside a vault, I realized, as I jerked my head around and tried to figure out how to see again.

There were cold, sterile metal walls everywhere. Pallets of boxes. A giant, thick door in front of me. Very much right in front of me. In fact, it was just inches from my nose. I could see the rest of the vault in the reflection of the overly polished metal as I turned my head back to face forward.

So I didn't need to scream anymore. The pain was gone.

I was whole.

I was alive.

"I'm alive!" I shouted and, startled to hear my own voice, I laughed.

I raised my hands up and my right arm made a ripping sound. I'd had it pushed forward, I remembered, a cold feeling rippling down my spine.

I had appeared right next to the wall.

Searing pain now ran up my arm, and I raised a stump. The end was cut clean off, like someone had just digitally erased it. Specs of silver wall flaked off.

And then the blood began to spray.

It was like something from the worst, cheapest horror movie ever. Blood. More blood. With every heartbeat.

My head swum.

And then instinct kicked in and I grabbed what remained of my arm, still shocked, and squeezed as hard as I could.

Pressure.

Pressure to stop the blood flow.

"Oh, this is bad," I kept muttering as I looked around.

There was nothing in here to help me. My arm was cut off and I was trapped inside a bank vault.

"This is bad."

I was squeezing, but there was still blood gushing out. I was leaving a trail of it as I staggered around.

"Not good." I couldn't even think of a swear word that covered something this bad.

I couldn't take my shirt off. I'd have to let go of my hand. Anything I could do to help would require letting go. And even if I did that for an instant, I had a gut feeling that it would be bad.

Could all this blood around me be mine? I was leaving footprints in it.

Sit down. Stop moving.

Think.

I was in a vault. What now?

Calm. I took a deep breath. That seemed to leave me dizzier, but the familiar act helped.

"HELP!" I screamed. "Alarms! Someone's in here. I'm stealing your valuables! Where are the cameras? Isn't anyone keeping an eye on this stuff?"

There were trillions of dollars of bits locked down here, right?

I bore down and thought, and then screamed, not in the real, but everywhere else.

Where was I?

It came to me. Deep under the ground. Miles and miles. Buried where the treasure was safest from attack. From everything.

Forget screaming being not-me. I was going to have to be heard if I didn't want to die after being transmitted across half the known universe.

I closed my eyes and cast about with the new technology in myself for anything that might help me.

I found a glimmer of a thread of something. My mind could sense a radio wave. A faint pip in the deep, deep dark hole I was. So I seized it and began to yank. Pull. Connect.

And then, like someone deep in the dark who found a tiny glint of sunlight at the end of a long tunnel, I shouted up it.

I screamed. In every possible way it was possible. I announced my presence, sent myself slithering off down that little thread. I hacked into anything I could find and destroyed it. Gave locations. Blundered around security systems.

Moving so quickly, and letting every little disturbance know that there was one place it was all coming from: me.

Me.

Down here.

My skin sizzled like a frying pan hit with water when my blood touched it. And something stored in one of the pallets nearby sparked and spat as the circuits died.

I was a broadcast beacon.

I was shining in the digital world, a personal lighthouse of come-and-find-me.

The giant door to the vault rolled aside. Bearings the size of fists squeaked as they moved tons of weapons-proof door aside.

Four men with guns moved quickly into the room and stared at me.

"Don't move!" one of them shouted.

"Who the hell are you?" another thought to ask.

Holding my bleeding arm up, I tried to stand, and failed.

In my calmest, most authoritative voice possible, I looked at them as I slid to my knees and announced, "I'm Jane Hawkins, one of the crew of the late sparship *Dorado*, on a treasure-seeking mission. I'm here to warn you about a possible attack on Earth by the *Sparkflint*. And I need medical attention. *Now*."

Something under my skin popped. I could smell burned skin. Blood dripped down my chin and out of my ears.

175

"Well that's not good," I muttered as they rushed to grab me under the arms and help. "Hey, you need to listen to me. I need to warn you about the *Sparkflint.*"

I kept repeating everything I could tell them until the rocky walls around me started to spin, and then waver. After that, words stopped making sense.

It got too dark too focus.

Chapter Thirty-Two

Something tickled the back of my neck. Rough pillow fabric, maybe. I woke up and blinked. And the tickling disappeared. I'd imagined it.

A man stood in the room at the end of my bed. He was flicking invisible things away in the air, his silvery eyes looking off into nothingness.

He wore a crisp, gray uniform. Epaulets on his shoulders. A pattern of insignia on his chest indicated someone important.

From deep within my own memory recognition blossomed.

This was a Captain of the Line!

Captains and Commanders of ships were linked. Not just to their ships and crew, like riggers. The Line was a way for commanding crew to add themselves into a command Consensus that used bits to communicate instantly.

The entire fleet would then have eyes and ears stretched out across light years. An entire fleet, swirling and swooping as one, spread out across entire star systems.

I sat up, and his eyes switched to focus right in on me. They weren't the crude eye-patches of the riggers, but silver eyeballs that reflected bits and pieces of the hospital room back at me.

"You're in Consensus right now, aren't you?" I asked, somewhat awed. Because bits were so expensive, Captains only created the Line when planets were under threat.

"We are," he said in a distant voice. "The Line is fully operational and engaged."

"I'm so sorry," I said. "I burned myself out trying to call for help. I can't give you code. I can't help you fight the *Sparkflint*."

The Captain smiled grimly. "That's okay, Miss Hawkins. Knowing there's a threat, and exactly what it is. Well, that's

often most of the battle. We have the *Flint* on the run, thanks
to you. Watch what happened just a few seconds ago."

Walls glowed as the Captain stabbed his finger at them.
Images of deep space flickered on as the walls rendered pieces
of what he was seeing on them. Battle reports. Images from
other ships.

At least five ships chased the *Sparkflint*. In most of the
images it was tagged with layers of data. Direction. Projections.
Tracking information.

Possible paths flew along in front of the spikey ship,
fading off on either side in line with assigned probabilities.
Then the lines jumped, this way and that. The old hull of the
Dorado shivered as the ship's spars twisted about. It was trying
to slip onto a new stream of energy. It was trying to escape its
pursuers.

Twinkling dust flashed and flared.

I was looking at a battle.

"It was surprised," the Captain said. "And it's now on the
run. And upset. And hurt…"

"How do you know that about its emotions?" I asked.

"It's not whole," he said. "The riggers made it out of
fragments and pieces of their minds. It's hatred, and lust, anger,
revenge and greed. We can hear it, on the edge of our
Consensus. And now it's gone…"

He waved a hand casually, all business now. The walls
faded back to boring white.

"Gone?" I asked.

"Damaged. Escaped. Limping away. More ships are
trailing it. We just dropped the Line. We don't need the full
Consensus. We'll leave those five ships to chase it."

The Captain walked over to the edge of my bed.

I could see that his eyes were fading into a deep blue
now. No longer silvery and reflective.

"There are going to be a lot of questions ahead." He set a
small printout gently on the bed next to me. "The things you
can talk about are listed there. Everything else… you'll do best
to avoid."

"There are things I can't talk about?" I asked.

"Quantum teleportation, for one. The real status of the *Sparkflint*. These are things we would… prefer to leave out."

"Then nothing makes any sense," I said.

The Captain smiled. "We will explain that you learned something from a rigger here on Earth, which led you to warn us that members of the original crew went to Thanatos to reawaken the *SparkFlint*."

"What about the vault, and those guards that saved me?" I protested.

"That never happened," the Captain said.

"But…"

"Never. Happened," he repeated. Then he sat down in the chair next to the bed. "Put your thumbprint on that document, and you'll have our support. And that is no small thing."

My left thumbprint. I looked at my bandaged right arm. There was a small, cup-like machine on the end of the stump of my arm, hooked to several wires.

I'd lost a piece of myself.

And I wondered if I was signing another piece of myself away.

The Captain nodded at my arm. "They'll grow a new one back for you," he said.

"But I can't afford…" I started to say.

But he just grinned. "We're sending a ship over to rescue your friends on Thanatos, now that we know where that is. I imagine, if what you told us earlier while being dragged out of the vault was true, that a bill won't be a problem. You'll have quite the finder's fee."

I looked over at him, not quite able to process that realization. And then I pressed my thumb to the paperwork in front of me. What else could I do, refuse the Navy?

"Whoever goes down to Thanatos to get them, can they do me a favor?" I asked the Captain.

"Of course," he said, picking up the document from my bedside and standing up to leave.

"Make sure they take down a selection of cheese for the crew down there," I told the Captain.

He looked befuddled. I kept my face calm and neutral, if not a little bit serious.

"Okay, Miss Hawkins," he finally said. "I'll make sure to do that. Any particular kind?"

"As big a selection as you can. Trust me, it's important."

"I'll pass it on," he said with a frown, but seeming to take my request seriously.

The door slid open to let him walk out. On the other side Sadayya stood, waiting. He nodded at her, and she very tentatively stepped in.

She had a pretty yellow headscarf on, unbrushed hair crazy loose around it, and horrible bags under her eyes.

"Hello mom," I said with a genuine smile. All these scheming people had filled my life for so long, I felt like the room melted when she stepped back in.

That was relief, I thought to myself, as she ran and grabbed me in a strong hug.

Against all odds, I was home again. And I couldn't have been happier.

Chapter Thirty-Three

With a gust of cold air the doors to our Inn slid open and a rigger stepped inside. He looked around, brand new black eye patches taking in the new marble floors of the lobby. He wore a synthetic cloak that kept adjusting itself, ruffling water droplets off the back and fanning itself out so that it would sit on his shoulders more comfortably.

I recognized the tats on his forearm without needing software to explain. I could see the resume written into his skin, I knew the sparships he'd sailed with.

But beyond that, I also recognized the rigger himself. I remembered him standing by Captain Garrik's side, protecting the crash site on Thanatos against Argyros's riggers.

"Miss Hawkins!"

"Mr. Lincoln Merriweather," I replied with a large smile as I stepped out from behind the reception desk. "Welcome. Are you here for the night?"

He looked around. "No. I heard you and your mother were still at the Inn, and I came by to visit you."

"This is all we have left of my mother, Tia," I explained. "When I came back, we knew neither of us wanted to give up her dream of having the Inn run just the way she'd wanted it, now that we have the... means."

Flying back over Sargasso with Sadayya, I'd looked down at the metal jellyfish shape of the floating city. It had seemed smaller, somehow.

But familiar.

Coming home, Sadayya's nervous hand on my new arm, had been comforting.

"I understand," Lincoln said. "And Armstrong, Woodgrove? They've dropped out of the public eye."

"Woodgrove got what she wanted out of me," I said,

maybe with a trace of bitterness. Most of the treasures on Thanatos had been returned. They had been stolen, after all.

I had enough to leave us and the Inn well off for life, now. All of us had gotten galactic-sized finder's fees.

Woodgrove had no further interest in us, though.

"Armstrong," I continued, less bitterly, "moved to one of the old cities somewhere."

"Good for the doctor," Lincoln said with a smile.

"And you?" I asked.

The old rigger smiled. "I sunk the money into the controlling share of a ship of my own. I'm a Captain."

I'd seen the Captain's marks on his forearm, but had wondered. "Congratulations," I said.

Garrik, I had heard, joined the Line, hunting the hull of his own ship. He'd never even bothered to come back to Earth.

There was one name still in the air, unsaid.

Lincoln fidgeted. "Argyros, you know he cut a deal to help the Line hunt the *Flint*, he came to see me in Canaveral not too long ago to ask for a favor."

I stiffened. "A favor?"

I hadn't seen or talked to him since Thanatos. Many of the others had visited me in the hospital.

Lincoln pulled a carefully folded scarf out of a pocket, and pressed it into my hands. "He said that I should give you this."

I looked at the scarf that had gotten me into so much trouble, and smiled as I ran my fingers down its edges.

"Thank you. It means a lot to me to have it back."

And, I wondered, how did Argyros know about the scarf? He was too clever for his own good, I thought.

"After the vault, your implants burned out," Lincoln said quickly. "Do you miss it all?"

I smiled, sadly. Lincoln nodded, his suspicion confirmed, and dropped the subject.

"It was good to see you, Jane. Good luck."

I wished him luck also. It was always a pleasure to see someone from the *Dorado*.

After he turned onto the street outside I shut down the desk and climbed the stairs.

At the second floor, I wrapped the scarf around my neck and slipped out the window onto the fire escape. I crawled up, though, from window to windowsill. I switched to climbing up the side of the drainpipe, quickly finding handholds and easily spidering my way up the side of the Inn.

In just seconds I vaulted to the top of the roof with practiced ease, my breath steaming as it hit the super cold, arctic air.

I liked the cold, now. It helped when I was pulling stunts like that, where I needed to move quickly and think fast.

Up here, on the solar tiles in the night, I had privacy and quiet. I could look far up over the roofs of Sargasso toward the stars.

Sometimes I woke up, screaming and drenched with sweat with the words 'pieces of meat' ringing around my ears, the image of blood everywhere fading away.

I thought about the feel of the Consensus a lot, and what it felt like to ride the controls of a spar. The howl of the winds between the stars, ready to be dipped into with a twitch of my mind, lurked around the edges of my mind.

I would miss all of it.

For now.

My skin came alive. The tracings of tattoos far below glowed blue, and then lit up the world around me. The sky filled with data.

I could see the ships invisible to the naked eye, riding up into orbit and beyond. Commercial chatter and sparship open channels filled the sky like auroras.

One day, I would buy a controlling share of a sparship for myself and go back out there. If the *Sparkflint* was still out there, maybe I'd even help the Line hunt it down. If not, I would explore the stars.

One day.

But not today.

"Jane?"

The Inn's systems I'd hacked told me that Sadayya was down near the lobby, looking for me. It was time for dinner, inside, where it was nice and warm. And, for now, good.

I jumped up and vaulted over the side of the roof.

The End

ABOUT THE AUTHOR

Called "Violent, poetic and compulsively readable" by Maclean's, science fiction author Tobias S. Buckell is a New York Times Bestselling writer born in the Caribbean. He grew up in Grenada and spent time in the British and US Virgin Islands, and the islands he lived on influence much of his work.

His Xenowealth series begins with Crystal Rain. Along with other stand-alone novels and his over 60 stories, his works have been translated into 18 different languages. He has been nominated for awards like the Hugo, Nebula, Prometheus, and the John W. Campbell Award for Best New Science Fiction Author.

He currently lives in Bluffton, Ohio with his wife, twin daughters, and a pair of dogs. He can be found online at:

www.TobiasBuckell.com

ACKNOWLEDGMENTS

This novel was a true passion project. It was not written with a proposal, or because I was asked to, but because I started reading a Project Gutenburg edition of *Treasure Island* on my iPad and realized that, as a kid, I had read only a 'sanitized' version. The real *Treasure Island* had an alcoholic pirate demanding that Jim Hawkins enable him in his attempt to drink himself into an early grave.

Struck by that raw image, I began to daydream about transhuman pirates with wetware and heat-transfer mohawks wandering into a future Admiral Benbow Inn. Jane appeared in my imagination, and suddenly I found myself writing a test opening chapter for fun. And then it kept going! I would read a chapter, and then write an answering chapter.

The further I got into this literary call-and-response the more fun I had and, quite suddenly, I found myself with a whole novel. Sure, I tweaked the end a bit, and cut out some bits, but this was the most fun I'd had writing in a long time.

Alas, Disney's own animated, somewhat science fictional take, *Treasure Planet*, meant that the project made it a hard sell even if an editor loved this book as much as I did.

And that was fair enough. Everyone right away asks if I've seen that movie. I have, but I had no thought about as I wrote this book, just a joy at seeing a new take on *Treasure Island* in space unfold as I wrote. Believe me, I only unearthed this book, I didn't plan it. Not at all.

As a result, I realized that going to my readers directly and seeing if this project interested them was my smartest move. They responded to my Kickstarter, funding the launch of this fun passion project you are now reading.

So I owe all of the following readers and backers of this Kickstarter a HUGE thank you:

The Trove

Chris Hyde
Kelly Naylor
Philip Reed
Mike Miller
Kerry Kuhn
Neil Clarke
Tim Moore
jfa82
David Chamberlain
Raph Koster
Howard Carter
D Franklin
Carl Rigney
Bruce
Nathaniel Lanza
Benjamin D.
Sparrow
Tristan Salazar
Pablo Defendini
Lawrence M. Schoen
Dan Rogart
Jon Lasser
James W Smith
Deniece Platt
Karen I Clark
joey
Andrew Hatchell
Deseree Stukes
David Garrett
Alex Ornelas
John Gamble
Robert Goldman
Erin Congdon
Manuel Garrido
Catherine Johnston
Dave Long
Spencer Gill
Chris McLaren

Stephen Boucher
Derek
John Wenger
Markus Fix
Kimberly Unger
Michael F.
Kristian Lundager
Matthew Caron
John Devenny
Xavid
Adam Roberts
Terry
Andrew Nicolle
Elyse M Grasso
Guest 351535440
Mary Agner
Bobbi Boyd
Jennifer Berk
Tony C Smith
Neil Muller
Michael Feldhusen
Tasha Turner
Kenneth Fields
C.C. Finlay
Derrick Eaves
Michael Breland
Cathy Green
jeremy
Stephen Jacksteit
Jeff Spock
Steven Halter
SeanMike
Jeff Gundy
Rob Eickmann
Chris Gerrib
Philip Proefrock
Mark Ames
Arne Radtke

Dennis Kuczynski
Clarissa
Phil Margolies
Kevin King
Lila Sadkin
Matthew Gaglio
Michael
Rae Carson
John Kovalic
keith miller
Todd Pollman
CJ
Agnes Kormendi
Camille Lofters
Mick G
Greg Levick
Scott Peacock
Frank Jürgens
Kemtae Lynch
Katherine Leah
Andy Taylor
Ian K Bruford
Drew Mac Donald
Cheryl Brandt
FiyazBhayani
Christopher Seman
Amirf
Shawn Posthumus
Karissa
Jeff Hotchkiss
Elizabeth B Bizot
Joem
Devin Ganger
Harold M Martinez
Garth Nix
AMD 'Doc' Hamm
Clare Bohn

187

Made in the USA
Lexington, KY
13 April 2018